Touch the Dead

E.S. Thornton

Fox2Rivers Books

This book is dedicated to my sister, Katherine, with love.

CONTENTS

Florida, July 2016

Eden's hair streamed with light as she moved through the water. This is where Jess had taught her to swim. She used to dive from the side of the old pier and follow her cousin underwater, longing for her child's body to grow sleek and beautiful, like Jess. As Eden swam along the seabed, the memory of Jess drew her away from the safety of the shore. When she reached the pier's end, she gazed beyond drifting sand and broken shells to where darkness waited. The currents were growing stronger, and she was cold. With aching lungs, Eden pushed up into the air and bodysurfed to shore.

From the beach she climbed wooden stairs to a walkway. She folded her arms on its splintered railing and gazed across the water. Clouds towered along the horizon. Far below the restless waves, schools of fish nosed among rocks and corals, floated past strange shapes encrusted with sea life, vagrant currents making a ghostly dance as they swept by. Little else threatened the distant reef's solitude.

Eden leaned down, and from a backpack she pulled on shorts and a T-shirt. She tied her shoes and jogged along the walkway over low shore dunes. They were covered with long-stemmed sea oats rustling in the wind. She reached the main road. Two miles south, she left the road to follow a winding drive beneath an archway of trees shaggy with trailing moss. Bright splashes of tropical plants and ferns grew thick in the moist earth, its scent rising in the damp shadows.

Ahead, a two-story building leaned against a slab of sky. Birds circled above the lodge's pitched roofs. Eden crossed the east porch and went inside to shower and change clothes before helping with dinner preparations for the lodge's handful of guests.

Later in the evening, after serving and clearing the table, she heard someone call the name "Eddie." It was the nickname he had given her when she was a tomboy lovesick from watching him dancing with Jess at the dunes. She hung her apron on a peg in the kitchen. She found him in the common room, a smile hovering at the corners of his mouth.

"You've been gone too long," Johnny said. His eyes studied her.

"Yes, it's been a while." Eden thought he must be able to hear the blood rushing through her veins. Walking over to him, she grew aware of the cigarette pack rolled in his sleeve, the muddy work boots, and the strangeness of being near him again.

"C'mon," Johnny said. His big rough hand gripped her own as they walked past the guests talking on the porch.

Outside in the parking lot, Johnny propped himself against the rear doors of his utility van. He hooked his thumbs through the beltless loops of his jeans.

"You're going to go looking for her." His voice was a near-whisper, as if these were words he hadn't wanted to say.

"I thought I might ask around. Why, is there a problem?"

Not meeting her gaze, he shook his head slowly, as if to say trying to find out about Jess, missing for close to three years, was hopeless, the challenges too great. He didn't say this. Not out loud anyway. But Eden was silent, thinking this is what he meant.

"You okay?" he murmured. His smile had returned. It was boyish and sad as he brushed a strand of hair from her cheek and cupped her face between his hands. She told herself not to let this happen, not yet anyway. Their lips met.

One of the guests walked into the parking area. The heart tattoo high on her cheek was like a bruise in the deepening light. She nodded at Eden and Johnny, her gaze lingering on him a moment longer before she opened the door to a pickup and climbed in. "Don't stop for me, you two," the woman called. But they had stepped apart. Eden was grateful to the woman.

She was followed by a raw-boned man in a plaid shirt. They were overnight visitors to the lodge from a town off the I-95 corridor near the Florida-Georgia state line. Johnny stared after their departing vehicle. As the pickup headed onto the main road, Eden asked Johnny if he had heard anything new about Jess. His phone buzzed.

Johnny moved off to answer, and she was unable to make out what he was saying. The short conversation ended, and he walked over to her. "Work. They want me," he said. He placed his hands on either side of her waist. "And I want you, Eddie. Stay with me tonight. I'll come get you later."

Eden looked at him wordlessly, hoping he would see she needed more time. He took her hand and bowed over it, a graceful, courtly guy who made her feel like a lady. When he pressed his lips to her fingers, she thought it might be a signal. He would be patient.

He gazed at her as he released her hand. "It's hard," he said. "But listen, you have to accept about Jess. It's a 'cold case.'"

As if from far away she heard her voice saying, "No, it isn't so," and Johnny calling out, "I'll catch you later." She watched him drive off fast into the dead heat of the night.

The glow of the taillights on Johnny's van disappeared around the stone posts at the lodge entry. She started up the east porch steps. There was cleanup work to do in the kitchen, but a short walk to the lake might help her sort out her feelings for Johnny. The lake was west of the lodge, its moonlit surface visible through a screen of trees and vines.

She heard a long splash, and she thought about 'gators and summers with Jess, Jess's twin Luke, and their friend Johnny, all of them going out in a rowboat to explore. The years had gone by. Jess was missing and Luke had died in combat in the Middle East.

And Johnny had left her feeling even more alone.

From the lake her thoughts traveled north to Illinois where she lived at the Blue Moon Trailer Park with her mom, Annie, until Annie's recent death. She had died in April of cancer after a long battle with the disease. There had been Annie's illness and Eden's struggles to save her brief marriage. It was not working out.

Looking at the lake and surrounding wilderness, she remembered the fox she'd come across last winter in the snowy Illinois woods. The wind touched the animal's red fur. It would never leap and run again.

The fox had gotten caught in her mind together with her missing cousin, Jess, and as she walked toward the yellow lights of the lodge, the fox and Jess moved along beside her through the darkness.

Chapter Two

The next morning a pickup truck rolled along the drive. When it had stopped near where Eden watched its progress from the east porch steps, she walked over to see what the stranger behind the steering wheel wanted. The window was down, and she found herself looking into a face pitted with small scars beneath a black watch cap pulled low over his brow.

"Can I help you?" Eden asked.

"I wanted to come by and pay my respects to Luke Sinclair's family," he said, slipping off dark glasses before introducing himself. McCabe Jones said he had served with Luke in the Middle East.

"I'm Luke's cousin, Eden. His mom isn't available, but I'm inviting you to have dinner with us." Aunt Billie was at her oceanfront cottage sleeping off too much beer and coffee brandy, and it could be she would show up if McCabe came over, but Eden wouldn't bet on it. She didn't see a need to explain any of this to him.

McCabe glanced at the lodge before settling his gaze on her. "Sounds good," he said. She thought she knew what McCabe saw: skin too pale for the blistering sun, a dusting of freckles across her nose, dark eyes shadowed underneath from lack of sleep, and finally he saw her lips. They were full and shapely.

"Luke and I were planning to surf together," McCabe said. He glanced along the drive toward the sea across the road. "He said a place near here was the best, and I thought I'd try it out. I'd appreciate it if you would give me directions."

"Two miles north, take the first dirt road off to the right. Follow it and you'll see a giant dune, a walkway, and an old pier. The break's good there." His eyes not leaving her face, McCabe slipped on his dark glasses with slow deliberation. He thanked her for the information and the invitation, and she watched him guide the pickup along the drive beneath the overhanging trees. He turned onto the main road at the stone entry posts.

Eden wiped a film of sweat from her face and neck, then, defying the intense heat, she took off running south along the road beside a flooded ditch. Weeds and feeding larvae grew in its brown water. Its surface rippled with the struggle of life and death. Before she had gone a mile, a pickup motored by. It pulled off a few feet ahead of her onto a grassy strip.

"Get in, Eden. It's too hot for a run, and it's close to lunchtime. I'll take you for some chow," McCabe called.

Eden detected in his manner a bossy quality she hadn't noticed earlier. She stared at him while thinking this over. He stared at her, too, his face unsmiling, and she realized getting in a pickup with him might not be a wise move. Still, the guy had spent time with Luke. Or said he had.

McCabe said, "Luke had a chipped front tooth and he usually had an unfiltered cigarette balanced behind his left ear." He reached over and opened the passenger door. With its banged-up, faded, and rusted exterior, McCabe's truck looked like it had been abandoned in a desert but was being brought back to life—it rode on a set of new tires.

She circled and peered inside. The interior appeared comfortable and clean. And lunch on someone else's dime was always good. She hoisted herself onto the seat, and told him where they could get burgers and fries. He eased onto the road.

McCabe glanced at her. She sat close to the door, ready to spring out if he did or said anything weird.

"Do you live at the lodge?"

"And work there. Housekeeping and kitchen duties for the summer." This was the length of time her aunt's boyfriend, Cap, said they could afford to pay her. She'd work, and she'd see what she could learn about Jess. Nobody could pay her for this.

"After summer's over?"

Thinking ahead took her as far as going back sometime to Illinois and the Blue Moon Trailer Park. Eden needed to sort through her mom Annie's belongings. Her heart wasn't in it, nor was she eager to track down her husband to see if he still wanted a divorce.

When she ran out of money, she could always get another waitress job. Start over somewhere new. It was in her blood, moving on.

Eden answered McCabe's question about her future with a shrug. "I'm not sure," she said. She studied his profile. He was older than Luke, probably close to thirty if not already there.

McCabe was saying, "Luke and I went on missions together. He told me about the lodge and the surfing around here. He was a fighter, Eden."

"Luke was in lots of fights," she said, remembering the broken front tooth and his bloody noses. He'd taught her to play poker, drink beer, and roll the occasional joint. Arm-wrestling and teasing figured into her relationship with him. Serving in the military, he had died doing what he believed in and was good at. There was some small comfort in this. But she couldn't find anything to give her comfort when she thought of Luke's missing twin, Jess.

She closed her eyes against the glare of the sun, and Jess came to her. She was at the dunes, her head lifted to the night sky as she brought a cigar to her lips, its burning tip moving to one side as she sipped from a can of Red Bull spiked with rum. Someone dared her, and she ran into the waves.

And vanished. Eden, in McCabe's pickup, remembered how Jess had reappeared on the beach, laughing, until she saw Eden's terrified stricken face, Jess holding her then. But Eden had felt something more than fear, and it was bitter as seawater. She had swallowed it down. The fact was Jess could have any man. And she had chosen Johnny, the one Eden wanted.

McCabe's voice broke into her thoughts. "Luke said he had a twin. He showed me a picture of her. You two could be sisters." Eden was almost twenty, the same age as Jess when she had disappeared from the lodge.

"What did Luke say about her?"

"He was going to come back and search for her." He stared straight ahead.

They had passed by an emergency care clinic and a supermarket before Eden said, "She could be out there still. Luke would find her." Eden fell silent. Neither said anything for a while.

McCabe leaned forward over the steering wheel. "One July Fourth my older brother had some firecrackers in his hand. I always did like he did. He lit his first."

"How bad was it?" Eden asked.

"Mangled a finger."

It was an invitation to share personal stories. Eden thought back to the social worker who had told her it was healthy to be open to people.

"Take some risks, share your life experiences, even the painful ones or those you might not be proud of. There may be rewards in being vulnerable," the social worker had said. But after thinking about it, Eden decided being vulnerable was for people who could afford it. No way was she one of them.

"Too bad about your brother," Eden said.

She caught sight of a surfer beyond McCabe's left shoulder. His outstretched hands scattered water and light like glass shards as he carved the green waves. Then he cartwheeled into the ocean. McCabe followed the direction of her gaze.

"Are you a surfer?"

"I haven't tried it in a long time. It can be tricky in Illinois. Winters especially."

"It wouldn't take me long to get you up on a board. There'd be no charge for lessons."

She searched his scarred profile for any hint of a smile. There wasn't one. She wasn't smiling either as she remembered falling from her board, the astonishing explosion of pain as her collarbone took the crack of it, the muscular swells dragging her under. Then Johnny bringing her into shore. He'd cradled her in his arms, and for the first time she had felt the pain of longing.

Over hamburgers and fries, McCabe jotted something on a scrap of paper and handed it to her. It was his number. "Add this to your phone. Call me if you want company when you talk to people about Jess."

He had an annoying way of issuing commands. "What makes you think I'm going to?"

"The bullets Luke took for the rest of us ended his plans to search for her. You're Luke's cousin. You'll follow where he can no longer go."

The pickup glided to a stop at the lodge. She gave him her number and had opened the passenger door when he pulled a small photo from his wallet, glanced at it, and offered it to her. It was of Luke going on a mission. She took the picture from him, and then she climbed down from the pickup onto the driveway. She walked up the east porch steps, aware of McCabe's eyes still on her, the faint sound of cards being dealt coming to her from far away and long ago.

She half-turned toward McCabe. "About surfing. I'll get back to you."

Chapter Three

Eden was brushing sand off her feet outside a cottage of weathered shingles when its front door, the color of faded lipstick, swung open. The woman at the door pushed a mop of blond hair streaked with gray off her face and with a cigarette in her hand motioned for Eden to step in. She walked into a shadowed room dominated by a window covered by a thin curtain. This allowed a blurred view of the ocean beyond. The furniture in the room stood at odd angles, as if the tide had washed in and hurried right back out. "You can go sit over there." Aunt Billie gestured toward a faded couch with torn upholstery shoved partway against a wall.

She went into a small kitchen. Returning with two glasses and a bottle of wine, she plopped down next to Eden. "So did you see Cap?"

"I did. He said he'd transfer the money to your account."

"Well, he hasn't, not yet anyway. I phoned once or twice to check." She snuffed her cigarette in a glass ashtray on a low table in front of the couch. "Actually three or four."

"Give him a bit longer."

Aunt Billie poured herself a glass of wine. She held the bottle toward Eden, who shook her head.

"Well, I've got other stuff, coffee brandy, beer, vodka." She squinted toward the picture window. Eden didn't get the feeling she cared anything about the view.

Aunt Billie frowned. "So he'll put the money in the bank. He didn't say anything else?"

"He asked you not to call anymore."

Aunt Billie's shoulders slumped. She gnawed a thumbnail.

Eden was hoping she wouldn't ask, but she did. "Was he with another woman?"

"He was."

"The lousy creep. She was young?"

"Yes."

"Well, all I can say is welcome to the club if she's going to be Cap's new little friend. There've been a string of girls, but I never burdened you about it." She gulped her drink and looked at Eden with mournful eyes.

Eden said, "Where do you keep tissues?"

"In the kitchen," Aunt Billie's voice trembled.

She found a box near the refrigerator. As Eden turned to leave, snapshots held with magnets to the refrigerator door caught her attention. The pictures showed her aunt dancing, reminders of when there were parties at the lodge and she was the hostess. There were photos of her in a bathing suit, in a ball gown, wearing a crown and sash and holding a bouquet. Her smile had been dazzling against her tan. These days her skin was like beef jerky. She'd been a Miss Magnolia Beach once.

Eden sat beside her aunt and set the box of tissues between them. Aunt Billie grabbed one, wadding it in her hand before reaching for a fresh cigarette from a pack and matches on the low table. She lit up and spoke through the smoke.

"You want something to eat?"

"What I'd like is to talk about Jess."

Her aunt flinched. Eden wondered if she'd been too abrupt in bringing up the painful subject of her missing daughter. But it was time to get to the point.

"I tell you what," Aunt Billie said, her tone along with a shoulder hike indicating she had no more than a casual interest in discussing her daughter's disappearance. "This whole business Jess started is what sent CJ to his grave a month or two ago, whenever it was, at the age of ninety-one or something. He wanted us to hire a detective. Couldn't afford one but the police have looked into it. There you have it in a nutshell." She lifted the glass and took a long sip. "CJ, though, you couldn't tell him she wasn't coming back."

"I'd like to hear about her last days, Aunt Billie. Was she upset about anything?"

Her aunt tapped the growing ash from her cigarette into the glass dish. She breathed with a wheezing sound as she gazed into the room's middle distance. "I've been feeling poorly for a few days what with Cap being so cruel. You and I can discuss Jess some other time when I am feeling stronger."

Eden stood up to leave. Aunt Billie wasn't quite finished talking.

"Do me a favor while you're cleaning CJ's place? See if you can turn up his war medals." She caught Eden's questioning look. Aunt Billie had never been interested in CJ's military history.

"Cap wants them for his collection." He was a veteran who raised money for veterans' causes. He also collected and sold military gear, guns, and medals.

"I thought you'd broken up."

Aunt Billie shrugged. "Cap will come back to me with the lodge being mine."

A memory came to her of a small box with its lid open, her grandfather seated at the kitchen table, his head bowed over the colorful ribbons inside. She and Jess had asked about the awards. The men he'd served with deserved them more than he did, their grandfather told them. He said nothing more before closing the lid.

"I will look around," Eden said.

Aunt Billie's eyes were fixed on her. "The way he liked to hide things, they could be anywhere," she said. "We've tossed out a bunch of stuff, but he may have left some unpaid bills. You be sure to bring me any papers you might find."

CJ never spent a dime he didn't have to, and his life was spartan. But she said, "I'll see what I can come up with." It appeared to Eden as if finding CJ's war medals was more important to Aunt Billie than seeking the truth about what had become of Jess.

Aunt Billie ground the cigarette in the ashtray and got up off the couch. Eden followed her to a door leading into the garage below.

They faced each other in the swarming shadows.

"I'm going to find out what happened to her, Aunt Billie."

"Who? Oh, for sure," she said with a dismissive wave. "If you want, you can take my car, swing by a garage first to have it checked for me? It has been running uneven ever since a fender bender I had a while ago. Pick up a quart of milk and some bread while you are out, and a pizza. If you want some, you can have it. Three cheeses with pepperoni on top. I'll reimburse you."

Aunt Billie opened the door to the garage and peered uncertainly down its stairs. "Car's old and beat up, like me," she said with a hard laugh. "A spare key's in the glove compartment," she said while closing the door.

Eden found the key, along with a small perfume atomizer and a Ladysmith .357 revolver wrapped in a cloth. Aunt Billie was prepared for romance or violence. Possibly both.

She inserted the key in the ignition. The Camry made a sound like her aunt's throaty wheeze. Then it died.

Chapter Four

Eden left the blinding light of the Florida sun behind as she stepped into a dark world of locked doors and disembodied voices. She identified those as coming from the town's emergency call center to her left. To her right, behind a clear plastic window, a woman worked at a desk. Eden walked to the window, and the clerk got up and came over to see what she wanted. Eden asked for a copy of the missing person report on Jess. The clerk told her the computer had been out of commission all morning.

"A technician's on the way."

"I can come back."

"Give me a minute. I'll see what I can do."

When she began to think the clerk had forgotten her, the woman returned with a printed report. It was four pages. Eden wanted to shout, "She's more than this. I loved her. You've got to help me find her."

She didn't shout. She stood there, and the clerk said, "There may be more on her, but until the repairman comes, I can't get at it. Anything else?"

Eden shook her head, and the woman told her what she owed. Fifteen cents a page.

The clerk returned to her desk. She removed a brown sweater from the back of a chair and slid her arms into it. She picked up a sandwich off a paper plate, tuna and mayo falling from between the crusts. Way too much mayo. Not enough tuna or relish.

Eden rummaged in her jeans for some coins. Her hands sweaty from worries she wouldn't have enough to pay for the copy, she counted out the change, and she took the report and walked outside, the smell of tuna following her.

There were dozens of cracks in the station's asphalt parking lot. Some of the cracks looked big enough to trap a hand or a foot. Heat rose from the cracks. Beyond, in a recreation area, kids were playing ball, and a lone skateboarder took a tumble, got up, dusted herself off, and tried again.

Eden sat on a bench, the shouts and sounds of the day melting into echoes of her cousin's laughter from long ago. She felt sick, but it wasn't the sick feeling a person can get with flu. It came from reading a report reducing her cousin to a few impersonal lines.

According to the report, Aunt Billie saw Jess for the last time at the beach near the old pier after the evening meal. She described Jess as defiant and belligerent, making demands when she had spoken with her about returning to the lodge. Instead, Jess had wanted more pay and time off to be with friends.

Eden looked up from the report and thought about what Aunt Billie had described as "demands." Jess wanted time to be with friends and to be paid fairly for her work? What an outrage.

She continued reading. Aunt Billie told the police even after several days had gone by she figured her daughter would show up at the lodge sooner or later. This is why she'd waited to file the report. Jess had not threatened suicide and had no physical or mental conditions placing her in danger.

Eden thought about the length of time it had taken her aunt to report Jess missing. People whose cats or dogs or pet snake went missing posted pictures and filed reports sooner than Aunt Billie had. Two weeks after the fact.

Aunt Billie had told her nothing. And so what she'd read sounded plausible.

Back in the station, she walked to the records window. The woman who had waited on her earlier eased out of her chair. Her body was big with all the breakfasts, lunches, and dinners she's made for the kids smiling at her from pictures on the shelf above her desk, meals for her brothers and sisters, cousins, nieces and nephews, her friends and extended family, and herself. Her body was generous with life.

If she were alive, Jess might become this woman, working in an office with family pictures set nearby so she could think about her relatives while doing other things like entering numbers in a book or filing reports. Such things weren't nearly as interesting as the family she'd have and the books she wanted to write. She'd wanted a china unicorn, too, like the one on the woman's desk.

"Can I help with anything else?"

"I want to talk with Officer Smith." Eden pointed to the name at the end of the report.

"Officer Smith's no longer with us." The clerk wrote something on a slip of paper and handed it to Eden. "Try Officer Campbell, but she's not in this week."

Eden walked along the road to the lodge. On the way a text message came to her. McCabe wrote: Surf lessons soon.

Eden didn't want to think about surfing and didn't send him a reply. She phoned her friend Kitty instead.

"I thought Jess's life was close to perfect. It wasn't." Even with Johnny.

"She wanted to shelter you from how hard life is."

"Still, she could have told me more. I guess I didn't know her."

"Eden, I suspect there were things she couldn't tell you or didn't know whether she should. But listen, if she was treated bad there at the lodge, her home, they might do the same to you. You should come back where you're wanted and safe."

"Safe? At the Blue Moon? Everyone drinks too much and shoots off guns and fireworks even when it isn't July Fourth or New Year's." Still, the trailer park was her home again since she and Ted were no longer sharing an apartment. When CJ was alive, the lodge had been a home for her for a few weeks during summers and other times, too.

The other night she had dreamed of CJ ordering her to find Jess and see to it he was buried at sea. He was angry at Aunt Billie for sticking him in the ground at the downtown cemetery. "Too much noise and traffic fumes. Leave it to Billie to do exactly what I told her not to do." The dream-conversation came to mind while talking to Kitty as she walked along the main road with the ocean to her right.

"Kitty, I can't leave here. Jess must be found. I owe the truth to CJ and Luke. They are my family, and they are still alive to me." Sometimes she'd hear Jess's laughter, and Luke rolling the dice. "And there's Aunt Billie, Johnny, even Cap. I want to find answers for them, too."

"Well, like I always say, don't trust anyone. If money is involved, those folks at the lodge are going to look out for themselves. Don't let appearances or their supposed ties to you fool you."

Kitty was an expert on appearances because of the so-called preacher, her ex-husband. He had always had a sunny smile and a warm handshake and something uplifting to say. Until the day he'd turned a gun on her and left her to bleed to death on the living room rug with the television on.

"But Kitty, even people with no evil intent to hide show each other masks most of the time."

"I didn't say it would be easy. Keep your eyes open for body language and listen for tone of voice. Do not dismiss the prickling sensation on the backs of your arms, either. With Clyde, I ignored all of it. He bought me a ring, and I thought I'd live happily ever after. I should've looked less at the ring and more at him."

"I'll remember the thing about appearance versus reality," Eden said. She asked Kitty to keep her eyes open for a lease renewal notice for the trailer she and Annie rented, and they ended the call.

At the east porch, guests Adele and Adam Winston along with Bobby Hayes, all of them carrying beach gear and reading material, trooped down the steps. They were laughing and talking. Adam gave her a long appreciative stare. Bobby, tanned and trim in khaki shorts and a Hawaiian shirt, gave her a shy smile. She exchanged greetings, and the three guests continued toward the sound of the surf across the road from the lodge.

Inside, Eden grabbed a duster, and rolled a vacuum to the guestrooms at the back of the lodge. She emptied a filled ashtray in Mr. Hayes's room, dusted a bedside table and retrieved from beneath it a book of matches, its cover printed with golden wavelets and the initials GC Hotel. She returned the cleaned ashtray and matchbook to the table.

Later in her room, she realized it was a seventeen-hour trip from Magnolia Beach to the Blue Moon by car with no stops. Bands of sunlight from the window moved across her backpack, like stripes on a highway.

Chapter Five

Eden had reached the lodge entry posts on her way to the road when a sleek black sedan with purple-tinted windows turned into the driveway. She glanced behind her, watching shadows slide off the sedan's Miami license plate as it continued between the lodge and toolshed. It stopped at Cap's place. In the short time she'd been at the lodge, she'd noticed vehicles going to and from his cabin. He was a gun collector and claimed to raise money for veterans' causes, although he never had made clear what those causes were. Thinking back to earlier years, she remembered Cap mostly slept late and hung out with Aunt Billie organizing parties. She didn't remember ever seeing the present amount of activity.

She'd turned south along the main road when a pickup slowed before pulling over and coasting to a stop beside the drainage ditch. Its window hummed down. "Hey, Eden," the driver called.

"We've done this before," she said.

"And it's almost lunchtime again," McCabe said. He leaned across the seat and opened the passenger door. "Climb on in."

As they neared downtown, a motorcycle came from behind so fast and close Eden thought it might take the Silverado's door right along with it. She watched as the Harley wove in and out of traffic before it cut away to the left onto a road leading to the Magnolia Beach Commercial Pier.

"Good thing we have guys like him to show the rest of us how to drive," McCabe said.

"I need to follow him."

"Who is it?"

"It's my aunt's boyfriend." According to a tearful late-night call from Aunt Billie, he still hadn't transferred the money and was continuing to ignore her calls, voicemails, and texts. Eden had agreed to speak to him again for her aunt. But she wasn't in any hurry.

McCabe let several oncoming cars pass by before making the turn leading to the pier. Eden left him searching for a space in the crowded parking lot while she headed to a ticket booth. The man who she thought was Cap had paused on the other side of the pier's entry gate after buying a ticket.

She moved in close enough to see the man's meaty profile. There was no question but it was Cap. He looked around at the crowded pier, searching for someone before striding along the wooden planks, the motorcycle helmet carried beneath his arm.

McCabe caught up with her and pulled some cash from a wallet for both their tickets. Eden thought of her neighbor Kitty telling her to find a man who didn't mind shelling out the big bucks for her. Kitty had lots of male friends, but she was still looking for a man with serious money. Eden had ignored what she'd said and married a guy who couldn't decide what to do with his life. She supported and encouraged him but he still hadn't figured out his calling when he'd left her. McCabe might be an improvement.

Eden walked along the pier, McCabe at her elbow, Cap moving on ahead.

The pier stretched a quarter-mile into the ocean. It was crowded with guys in stained T-shirts and ball caps. They'd brought along wheeled carts loaded with gear and hopes for catching something to eat or boast about, something to show for the day instead of the usual haul from the streets of hard knocks. Their fishing rods trailed lines in the green water.

"The aunt's boyfriend. Has he done something other than demonstrate he could benefit from a refresher driver's ed class?" McCabe asked.

"It's what he hasn't done. My aunt says he owes her money, and so far he's not paying up."

Overhead, gulls were doing a lot of shrieking, and she thought Cap might glance toward the feathered commotion and see her hair blazing in the sunlight before she had made up her mind whether she wanted him to recognize her. The loud birds sailed off, and Cap stepped in beside a man cutting into a fish with a knife.

There was a breeze, though not enough to dislodge the other man's cowboy hat. He pushed the hat up, revealing his face instead of menacing gunslinger shadows. Eden knew who he was. His attention was on Cap, and she didn't think he'd seen her.

McCabe tilted his head in the direction of the railing where Cap was propped on an elbow facing the other man, his back to them. "You were speaking of your aunt and the boyfriend. Do you know who he's with?"

McCabe and Luke had served together, he'd said. He was taking her to lunch again, he was good for a ride, and there was the offer of a surf lesson or lessons. Eden figured he was useful. She was beginning to feel reasonably comfortable talking with him.

"Cap's talking to a guy who was friends with Luke and Jess. You remember where I said you should go for the best surf near the old pier? People sometimes call the area the fox dunes. We used to party there with him. His name's Scooter."

Foxes hunted in the dunes wilderness and along the shore. Rain and moonlight caught in their fur, their yellow eyes watching the world from behind twisted trees and tropical plants with fiery leaves. She and Jess used to see their ghostly shapes moving through the shadows in the early morning and late at night. It had been magic.

She forced her attention back onto the pier where Scooter and Cap were talking. Whatever reason had brought Cap here, it didn't seem to be fishing.

At the dunes when Johnny didn't have his arms around her, Jess danced with Scooter. He knew all the latest moves. And wherever Scooter was it was sure to be the center of interesting conversations if not outright events and suggestions as to where the action would be on following nights.

Eden and the others were excited whenever he'd pull into the clearing to show them the newest set of wheels he was driving. It was understood he'd be moving on at any minute to party with an older crowd. Except Scooter usually wound up staying. Because of Jess. He would do anything to make her his. This was plain from the way he watched her.

The hissing waves and crying gulls were joined by a sudden harsh expletive as Cap stepped away from the railing. He turned on his heel, so riled he wouldn't have stopped for Eden even if she had rushed over and planted a kiss on his bloated cheek. She watched him head toward the gate and parking lot. There he climbed on the Harley and strapped his helmet under his chin, then tore onto the street and into heavy traffic.

Eden said, "More about Cap. We grew up hearing his war stories and looking at the military gear he's collected and sells. My aunt used to ride on the back of his bikes."

Aunt Billie laughing and holding onto Cap, the two of them would roar out of the lodge driveway on a fancy chopper, her dirty-blond hair flying. Those had been the good days for the former beauty queen before tequila shots and hangover cures on the beach became a daily habit.

Cap had departed and Scooter continued slicing. The fish-cleaning table where he worked was equipped with a spigot and a drain emptying into the ocean. A cigarette dangled between his lips. He leaned against the cutting table, his wrist flicking as he thrust his knife deep into a fish belly. Eden walked over to him.

Chapter Six

He stared sideways at her from behind dark glasses, light spilling off the blade of his knife. He set it aside. He reached for a small rag and slowly wiped his hands. A gold stud gleamed from his earlobe; a gold chain hung around his neck.

"Hello, Scooter."

He removed the cigarette from between his lips and tossed it into the ocean. Grinning, he leaned an elbow against the table. "So where have I met you before, little lady? Were you ever on a trip to the Caribbean?"

Eden said, "I used to see you at dunes parties."

"Shoot," Scooter said. "You don't expect me to remember anything from the dunes? You're going to have to help me out."

"I'm Eden, but it felt like I was Cinderella the night you danced with me." Flattery could sometimes get a person what they wanted. Besides, there was truth in it.

The night when she'd danced with Scooter, she'd been working hard to tear her eyes away from Johnny, with little success. Suddenly Scooter was at her side. They had danced fast and slow and in between, and for a while the empty, cold feeling of being alone had left her.

She had believed she wasn't always going to be a lonesome freak with her flat chest and skinny arms dangling for all the world to see her shame in her looseness, her lonely condition. Her heart wasn't always going to be in ragged pieces over Johnny belonging to Jess, and their being together wouldn't gnaw at her the way it did until she was half-crazed with longing and confusion because she loved Jess. And wanted Johnny.

"I made you feel like Cinderella?" Scooter tilted his head, and she felt the heat of his gaze from behind his dark glasses lingering on her mouth.

"Right, you did."

"Well, Miss Eden, how about we do it again?" He tipped his hat. "You and me, we'll dance at the dunes. What do you say?" His voice had a pleasant nasal burr to it.

Eden was about to tell him yes but she had lost track of McCabe, and it had distracted her. The feeling of being left behind made her flash back to her husband leaving her at Walmart. It had been way too far to walk with bags of groceries to the Blue Moon Trailer Park in cold so fierce the bananas would have all turned black. Kitty had come to get her.

She looked around. McCabe was a few feet away, watching her.

Scooter reached into a pocket and removed a business card. He handed it to Eden. "I didn't get your last name," he said. She looked at the card. Scooter operated Magnolia Adventures, a fishing charter and eco-tourism business.

"I didn't give it. It's Sinclair. Eden Sinclair."

Scooter's face broadened in a wide smile. "Well, I'll be damned. I was thinking, 'She sure does remind me of someone from out of the past.' And I was right." He drew her to his side, releasing her when McCabe walked over. She introduced the men.

"You must be staying at the lodge?"

"Yeah. Working there."

He lit a fresh cigarette, blowing a stream of smoke while he studied the deck. "It's a terrible loss, the two of them." He glanced at McCabe. "Did you ever meet Luke and Jess?" He gave McCabe a business card.

"I was with Luke in the Middle East." McCabe slid the card into his back pocket without looking at it. "He told me about his sister," he said.

"We all used to party together. You'd never want to try and tell Jess to do something. And Luke, he was a quiet guy until he got mad. I wouldn't have figured him for a hero, but I heard he died saving his men."

"He did," McCabe said.

"You were there? Bodies and blood everywhere, mayhem, huh?" The request for details and description didn't sit well with McCabe.

Scooter swiftly changed the subject. He said to Eden, "Back in the day it was fun being at the lodge, you know what I mean?"

"I'm interested in your recollections," Eden said. A seagull flapped in close to have a look around, its sturdy legs and webbed feet extended. The seabird landed with a bounce and walked along the deck, eyeing Scooter, and the fish. When the bird saw the problems involved in grabbing the fish from the cutting table, it spread its wings and flew off. Eden had been silently rooting for it to get the food.

"This one time Johnny, Luke, and myself hot-wired Cap's old Chevrolet. You might've seen him? We had a bit of an exchange of words."

"What about?" Eden asked.

"Business," Scooter said, waving a hand downplaying its importance. "Stuff with Cap, whatever it might be, so far it has always blown over between us. Anyway, he sneaks up and wrestles the Chevy's door open and aims a gun at us. Unless we get the hell out, he's going to maim each one of us for life. We bailed although not in a hurry because his old car has the worst doors for sticking than any I've ever experienced.

"But Jess, well it made no difference to her Cap's being a decorated veteran and hero. She sashayed off in the way she had, taunting him. And him with a gun." He blew some smoke, his glance traveling to Eden's mouth. "I tell you what, she was one great little gal. And here you are for all the world her double, I swear. A few years ago, anybody hearing you were related would've laughed out loud."

Eden didn't feel it necessary to respond. Despite the insult, she was glad for not chasing after Cap, having stayed instead to reintroduce herself to Scooter. He had spoken about the world he and Jess inhabited, and he might have more stories to tell. Ocean swells hit the pilings, and the pier shivered beneath her feet. It felt like a warning.

Scooter rubbed the back of his neck. "It could be Miss Billie was more interested in having fun with her guests than raising kids," he said, "which could account for Luke and Jess being as wild as they were. Jess especially, running off the way she did."

Scooter had revealed a talent for amateur psychology, but how far to trust what he'd said was another matter.

"What's your evidence she ran off?"

The hot sun burned. And she sensed him growing distant, like a fishing line moving out to sea. He was thinking how to respond, taking his time. "About your cousin. I'm not telling you something new, but they've investigated, and they haven't come up with a body."

"So because there's no body, you think she's out there still?"

McCabe, studying the swells rolling into shore, moved closer to listen to what was being said. At the same time a call came for him, and he stepped away, his head down as he spoke with the caller.

"Don't you believe what they've been saying about Johnny these last few years. Remember, the cops have found nothing they could ever pin on him. They questioned him a long time, too. A real long time and more than once. He's a good guy, never hurt anyone, at least I never heard of it, and he never would, except for occasionally punching someone out. He can get pretty worked up about stuff, and he has those big hands. He and Luke were both real hot tempered."

Eden understood Scooter's meaning when he referred to "what they've been saying about Johnny." She had watched true crime television shows with her mom and neighbor Kitty many times, and it was nearly always the husband or boyfriend who murdered the wife or girlfriend.

"She ran off, pure and simple," Scooter was saying. "What happened next?" He shrugged and spread his hands wide in a universal gesture showing he had no idea. "Anyway, anytime someone says something about Johnny and Jess, I say to them 'she ran off.' You will hear things about Johnny. I'm doing you a favor telling you."

An image came to her of Johnny as he had been when he moved into the lodge, his hair tousled by the wind, all elbows and stumbling close behind his friend Luke from middle school. And then years later, his muscled arms pulling her from the waves. Johnny was her first love the moment she saw him. What Scooter had said was like foam scuttling across the sand, not attaching to anything. She'd never believe Johnny was capable of seriously harming anyone.

It had all been smooth the way Scooter had spoken of Jess, saying she'd run away without offering any evidence to back up the claim, then introducing Johnny's name, insisting Johnny had no role in the disappearance. But the way Scooter did this suggested Johnny was guilty. She had a feeling he knew more than he was letting on. But it was only a feeling.

"Did they question you, Scooter?"

He grinned. "Me? Oh sure. They came up empty." Scooter caught a fish and slapped it alongside the one already split open on the cutting table. He pushed a mound of entrails to a drainpipe, Eden watching as the innards slid from the mouth of the drain into the ocean below.

Scooter said, "Nothing going into the water from here ever reaches the bottom."

He thrust his hands under the spigot to wash away the fish guts and blood clinging to them. The way he kept staring at her, she wondered if, because of her line of questioning, Scooter could be trying to send her a message with what he'd said. She would ignore the message.

Before leaving, she asked him for names of people to talk with about Jess. "You should be able to reach them," he said, mentioning two men. As he spoke, he lifted his dark glasses to look at her. Thinking about eye color was a hobby with her. Johnny's were the color of worn sea glass. McCabe's were the deep blue of a mountain lake. She couldn't tell the color of Scooter's eyes.

She found McCabe leaning against his pickup. He was talking on the phone while watching her as she came toward him. She kept her eyes on him, too.

He was attractive in a hard and scarred way, and she had a beautiful mouth and a good enough body, but she didn't need any more entanglements than she already had with her husband and Johnny. Besides, McCabe was too old for her.

He stopped at a place where they ate burgers and fries and consumed chocolate shakes, McCabe paying, then drove north along the main road to the lodge. McCabe told her he expected to come back to town in about ten days. He'd give her a surf lesson then. He named a specific day of the week.

"Mark it in red on your calendar," he said.

"Like it's a national event."

"I'll bring a board for you," he said. He paused before glancing her way. "And donuts." He instinctively knew her weaknesses.

From the porch steps she watched the Silverado make a slow turn north at the stone posts. She found Ruth at the back of the lodge in the kitchen. It didn't take long before the conversation between them moved from what the elderly lodge manager wanted her to do about dinner preparation to centering on Jess.

"What have you found out?" Ruth asked.

"Nothing. But I'm working on it."

***

At the end of the drive, Eden turned left and continued along the main beach road. It would be good to work off the burger and shake with a run. She had remembered a face and name from those dunes parties and had already used her phone to visit several websites. She hoped to find the woman still living in Magnolia Beach. It hadn't taken long before the woman turned up. She worked at a popular seafood restaurant at the north end of town. Along with pictures of her at the restaurant there were pictures of her in underwater diving gear. Eden remembered the woman hanging around with the dunes crowd. She never saw her dance with anyone. Not even Scooter. Her eyes were always on Jess.

From the outside, the restaurant looked like something left behind by a particularly violent hurricane. Inside, it was dark and cool and mostly empty except for a couple of men at the bar and a guy collapsed in a corner with his head on a table. The place smelled of stale beer and frying food.

She had stopped to glance at fish feeding in a lighted aquarium, the restaurant's one bright spot, when the woman she hoped to talk to materialized at the bar. Eden left the aquarium behind and crossed the room. The woman exchanged a few words with the men hunched over mugs of beer and walked to where Eden was perched on a bar stool.

"You're underage, darling."

"It all depends, doesn't it, Meg? I'm Eden Sinclair, Jess's cousin. You remember her? Coffee would be good. No milk. No sugar."

Their eyes hooked, and Eden decided Meg looked like a doll with her rosy cheeks, long lashes, and round bright blue eyes.

Meg nodded in the direction of a table near a window. Beyond it a wide river rolled to the sea. "Meet me there." Not long after, she came over with Eden's coffee and a glass of chilled white wine for herself. She set the coffee and her drink on the table before swinging a chair around, hoisting a dainty tattooed leg over the seat, and settling in with her arms resting across the chair back. Her T-shirt gave off the strong odor of bacon grease.

"Your cousin and I were lovers," she said.

Chapter Seven

There were any number of things Meg might have said, but Eden hadn't expected to hear she and Jess were lovers. It was possible Meg said what she had merely to shock her. Why Meg would care to do this wasn't clear to Eden, and she thought it could be a matter of personal style, Meg finding it amusing to cock her head and say something provocative so she could watch how people reacted. Eden was not above doing this. Whatever the case, another person's sexuality was not a big deal, not to rational people anyway. Still, what Meg said got her attention. Jess had never hinted at a romantic relationship with a woman, and Eden had to admit she was jealous. If what Meg said was true, her cousin hadn't felt close enough to her to share the information. But Meg could be lying.

Eden sipped her coffee, letting the idea of Jess with Meg find a place in how she wanted to approach talking with her. She said, "Jess never told me."

Meg said, "Yeah, well, we kept it to ourselves," and she shifted her gaze to the tabletop. Eden thought Meg might want from her simple recognition. But what kind? Telling Meg Jess had loved her? Eden couldn't answer this.

"Tell me about you both being divers."

Meg nodded, the corners of her mouth softening somewhat. This slight change in expression signaled a lot, which is how it often was with little things. Still, she wondered how much she'd have to work at getting Meg to loosen up.

"You ever dive with her?" Meg asked.

"Jess said I'd need lessons before she'd take me. I've gotten a certificate since then." Eden went to the local pool for lessons after Ted decided they might go diving on a honeymoon in the Bahamas. They wound up at a tropical-themed motel in Chicago featuring fake palms in the lobby and a heated over-chlorinated swimming pool. The only fish she saw decorated the plastic shower curtain in the bathroom. The fish were attractive and colorful.

"We used to go to Red Parker's Reef," Meg said, looking downriver to the sea.

Jess had never said much to Eden about the reef other than pointing it out when they went to the beach.

"It's offshore not far from here, right?"

"About ten miles east from the fox dunes. We'd go about seventy-five feet to the seabed and explore the wrecks." Eden wondered if Jess hadn't spoken of the reef at any length to her because she didn't want Eden nagging her about it. She hadn't talked about Meg or the reef because both were tricky subjects.

As she spoke of the reef, Meg leaned forward over the chair back, her face thrust toward Eden's. "We can go sometime if you want," she said. There was a light in her voice and face, as though Meg believed if she went to Red Parker's Reef she might find Jess waiting for her there. Eden understood the feeling, given her own strong wishes to be with Jess again and how much her cousin loved the water.

"I can show you where we used to go so you can see the place she liked most. I want to take more photos."

Wreck diving. Eden could feel herself wedged in a cramped space, sharp protruding things slicing into her air hose like a knife through soft butter, darkness closing in. She held her coffee mug with both hands, concentrating on keeping the liquid from slopping over the rim. When she finally spoke, Eden told a half-truth: "I'd like to go on your next dive."

Meg nodded. "With me, Jess was happy. No one could take anything from her when we were diving together." She looked out the window in the direction of the sea.

"People took from my cousin," Eden said. "What did they take?"

Meg's face tightened. "At the lodge she was a kind of cash register for her mom and the mom's gross boyfriend. They wouldn't let her keep her tips and they didn't pay her much. The boyfriend came on to her sometimes, too." Meg flexed her fingers.

Eden froze.

"She knew I'd kill him if he laid a hand on her and I found out, so she never said much of anything about it, but yeah, they used her. She was young and wanted approval. She tried to seem sure of herself. But she wasn't strong."

Memories came to Eden of Aunt Billie mocking Jess, her hair, her looks, Aunt Billie bringing home clothes from fancy stores while Jess wore secondhand outfits. And there had been those command performances where Jess and Eden had to dance for guests or with them when a guest didn't have a partner.

Eden shifted on the chair. The coffee tasted burned.

"A few people other than me helped and supported her, CJ, and Luke mostly, but CJ was sick and old, and Luke was off being a guy." She hesitated. "Also, Johnny wasn't there for her as much as he could've been."

"What do you mean?"

"Johnny's all about himself more than anything, and it's easy to understand why. He thought he'd found a lasting home at the lodge, but this is nothing new to you."

"I'd like to hear your view."

"You'll agree he needed a home and he had one at the lodge, for a while at least. It wasn't ideal. From what I heard from Jess, he'd never been paid what he should've been for all the maintenance and gardening and tree work he did there, but at least he had food and a bed, and a family in Luke and Jess and the woman who runs the place."

"Ruth."

Beyond the window, pelicans and gulls stretched battered wings to the sun. When Luke brought Johnny to the lodge, Luke had told Jess and Eden about Johnny living in the dunes wilderness with a monster pretending to be human. "Johnny didn't fear snakes or alligators," Luke said.

From what Luke told them and from Johnny's silence Eden understood it was the human with an empty shallow grave in the place where a heart should be, the human monsters among us who were dangerous, who made life intolerable, not the wild creatures in the forest.

Meg sipped her wine. "Johnny's plans for getting himself a permanent home at the lodge came apart when Jess ditched him, or so the story goes. She had had enough. He'd gone off with other girls too often."

"I remember them splitting and getting back together more than once," Eden said. Each time she'd get her hopes up. Each time he'd return to Jess.

She glanced beyond the window at the river gleaming bronze in the sun. She felt its currents pulling her out to sea. It carried her along with Jess and the fox. They had been caught together in Eden's mind, and they swam beside her in the bronze river currents.

She put the mug of coffee aside and rubbed her hands across the tops of her jeans, then folded them together, setting them before her on the table. She leaned in against the table edge.

"And after each breakup, from what I remember, he'd go right on living there at the lodge. What changed?" Eden asked.

"They say she gave him an ultimatum, and it enraged him. He killed her over it. She disappeared soon after the breakup."

"Did she tell you any particulars about what happened with Johnny?"

"She was prideful, keeping things to herself. She told me it ran in the family."

"What do you believe happened to her?" Eden was asking this question a lot. At some point someone would reveal the truth.

Meg lifted a shoulder. "Sometimes I think Johnny did her in. He was crazy about the lodge, more so than about Jess, if you ask me. Neither one of them was exactly what you'd call stable, but he had more to lose."

Meg walked her fingers through a wet ring on the table. "There's been some talk about Jess dying because of an accident at sea. Some say Johnny covered up the accident because of something in his past he feared would implicate him in her death. You hear Johnny's name a lot in connection with her disappearance."

"It sounds like you don't think much of him."

Meg stared at Eden, her eyes suddenly sharp, her expression challenging. "She loved me. She did." And then her eyes filled with tears and she balled her hand into a fist and brought it down on the table with a soft thump.

"Effing crazy world," she whispered.

Meg had said she and Jess had been lovers. Eden couldn't talk to Jess about any of it.

"You say Johnny's unreliable." Eden wouldn't have thought of him as any more unreliable and selfish than other guys. Those traits sometimes came with the territory along with doing stupid things, but in fairness, guys didn't have a corner on the market. Women weren't immune, she would be the first to admit. But she wasn't talking with Meg in order to rush to Johnny's defense. She wanted to hear what Meg had to say.

Meg's fingers pushed through more wet spots on the table. "She told me he'd go off and leave her when they went diving sometimes. Same thing happened at parties. She'd look around for him, and he wouldn't be there. It didn't hurt his reputation, though. Women want to feed him and love him. Johnny's always taken care of."

Eden remembered a girl with long silky hair who used to come to the dunes with Scooter. She'd keep her eye on Johnny, and he'd dance with the girl with silky hair if Scooter managed to cut in on him and Jess. She wondered if the girl was one of the ones who took care of Johnny. She had a sense she was related to Scooter.

She described the girl. "Any idea who she is?"

"It's Kathy, Scooter's sister. She runs a fancy beauty salon and spa downtown and is doing real well. Lots of customers. I should get myself a manicure there one of these days." She laughed and glanced toward the river, her face coloring, and she patted her hair, examined her nails. Eden decided Meg was somewhere in her mid-thirties. "Jess was friends with Kathy, by the way. You might want to talk to her.

"Anyway, Scooter's boat is usually moored out there. It's in dry dock. An engine fire, I heard."

Meg told her it was at least forty feet or more in length, a big vessel. "Fishing charters must pull in top dollar," Eden said.

"It could be he has more than a few ways of making money. An entrepreneur." She tapped her fingers on the table and stared at Eden.

At the dunes, Scooter used to move off from the crowd, one or two kids following him into the shadows as though the shadows were his office, money changing hands, all of them doing business with Scooter. Everyone knew what it was about. It was no big deal unless the police were cruising the area.

Eden nodded. "Do you believe Scooter might've had something to do with her disappearance?"

Meg shrugged. "Jess didn't want anyone or anything controlling her. She managed to stay friends with him for some reason I never did understand. She liked to dance with him," she said.

"He used money and drugs to try to control her?"

Meg nodded. "He tried with money and dope, yes. He promised her instant fame if she'd let him take pictures of her, post stuff of her on the internet. She wanted to be someone, but not the someone he wanted her to be."

She glanced in the direction of the window, some memory coming for her from off the river, making her doll's face grow even more sad in the late afternoon light. "I could always be wrong," Meg said in a near whisper.

Meg finished the last of her wine, set the glass on the table, and Eden thought she was going to end the conversation. Meg hesitated, frowning.

"We fought sometimes, and if she didn't have to be back at the lodge, she'd go hang out for a while at Harbor Place for somewhere to go."

"Harbor Place?"

"It's a homeless shelter west of the commercial pier downtown. She'd go there sometimes and volunteer in the kitchen."

Eden filed the name away for a future visit. She asked Meg if she thought Jess might have gone with friends from the shelter to California or South Dakota or Vermont to make a new life.

"Could it be she doesn't want to be found by anyone from around here?"

A jagged light came into Meg's eyes, and Eden thought this conversation between them must have disturbed the reef of dreams and memories of her and Jess together. She probably regretted talking with Eden.

Meg curled her fingers into a fist. "She wouldn't run off, leaving me. Not my baby girl

Jess." She straightened her fingers, inspected them with a frown.

Meg changed the subject.

"So, you're a diver?"

Eden looked around to see if she might be addressing somebody else, because she didn't think of herself as any such thing, not even remotely. As he gave her a certificate at graduation, her diving instructor had gripped her hand and urged her to be careful. It left her feeling shaky.

"Not counting the swimming pool where I took lessons, I've dived a couple of lakes."

"Lakes?" Meg made a scornful face. "The reef is for experienced divers, but I'll keep an eye on you. It's a place not too many get to see. It was Jess's favorite place."

Eden told herself it was the wretched coffee making her insides roil, but thoughts of getting lost, of being left behind were upsetting her more. She had seen a movie about a couple on a vacation in the Caribbean. They went on a dive with a big group. Nobody noticed they weren't on board for the return trip to shore. They were never found.

Meg had mentioned the theory earlier, about Jess meeting with an accident at the bottom of the sea. Eden visualized sand swirling around Jess's outstretched arms. And around her own. She gave herself a silent lecture about being positive. After all, she had earned a certificate. It stood for something, and diving with Meg she'd be with someone experienced. Longing to see the places Jess had visited, wanting to test her own ability, these were working on all her fears the way tides erode the barrier of the dunes.

"How often do you go to Red Parker's Reef?"

"Every couple of months. We were almost always alone there. Like I said, it's remote. Jess wasn't afraid, though." Eden gave Meg her phone number. Late afternoon drinkers were beginning to drift to the bar. Meg went over to serve them. On her way out, Eden stopped at the aquarium. It was by a wall near the door. The fish were feeding.

"Jess loved to watch them," Meg said. Eden hadn't sensed her come up. She stood close to Eden.

"See those?" Meg pointed above the aquarium at the wall behind it. Eden hadn't given any attention to the photos pinned there when she came into the restaurant. The wall was in semidarkness.

There was an enlargement of a diver poised near the propeller of a submerged aircraft. The girl's face was obscured by a mask, mouthpiece, and hoses. Still, from the flowing hair and something in the way her body was poised in the instant the picture was taken, Eden knew this was Jess.

"She said her grandfather would like to visit the old airplane if he ever went diving. There was no chance of this happening. He'd been sick a long time, she told me. Anyway, it was her favorite place, maybe because of her grandfather. Look, I have to go. I'll see you later." Meg moved off toward the bar.

A cold draft of air at her back, Eden left the restaurant and stepped into the harsh glare of the Florida summer. A crow called from up high in the brown fronds of a palm. She half-expected the bird to drop straight down to the pavement, struck dead by the piercing rays of the sun. The ragged spirit flapped away.

She pulled out dark glasses and inspected the plastic frame embedded with rhinestones. They were glittery and pretty, and they made her think of Jess. Eden had found the glasses on the beach. She blew sand from the hinges, and she slipped the glasses on and started toward the lodge.

The sports car zoomed by near enough for her to feel the heat of it before it pulled off the road and came to a stop ahead. The passenger door opened with a flash of gold bracelets, and she saw a wide grin below the brim of a cowboy hat shadowing the eyes beneath it.

Chapter Eight

He didn't wait for her to fasten her seatbelt before he'd shifted into high gear, throwing her against the seat back.

"There's this thing they say about seatbelts saving lives. You ever heard it?"

"Sorry," he said and stepped on the gas.

She could add reckless disregard for others to the list of what Meg had said about Scooter. In fairness to him, though Eden wasn't inclined toward fairness at the moment, Meg may have been trying to throw a cloud of heavy suspicion his way. Eden reminded herself she needed to keep on listening and not jump to conclusions.

"Do you think the food's good at the marina?" Scooter said. He'd probably been checking on his boat repairs and had seen her emerging from the restaurant. Still, it was clear he was fishing around as to what had taken her there.

"The coffee's atrocious. I haven't tried the food."

"Their fried shrimp is local and tasty."

"How's your boat? I heard there was a fire."

The smile faded. "Who told you?"

"Meg." Meg didn't need any further identification. Scooter would have stopped off at the bar for a beer and a meal every so often. And she'd been a fixture at the dunes parties.

"Meg." Scooter laughed, a common strategy to put down another human being at mention of their name, the laughter serving to say the other person is a clown and not to be taken seriously. "She's a real character, nosey if you ask me. In my opinion, the job doesn't keep her busy enough."

"I heard you're real busy, Scooter, with fishing and a few other lines of work. I heard you don't need to worry about money for repairing your boat."

His face flushed. He stared across the seat at Eden, his smile lazy, self-satisfied. "I won't deny life's good." He glanced in the mirror. "I could help make improvements in your life, too."

"Well, Scooter, the offer comes at a time when I'm interested in self-improvement in a major way. So tell me what you have in mind."

"I'll need to talk to a few people first, see what they say." His board of directors, no doubt.

Several miles along he swung into a sharp left turn. The engine slowed as they lurched in and out of potholes along a dirt road. On either side live oaks spread heavy limbs hung with streaming gray moss.

Ahead was a small clearing and a wooden walkway. Pickups and vans were parked in the clearing. The walkway led past a towering dune on the left across a shallow valley and low shore dunes to the beach. What was left of a pier teetered into the sea. This was where Jess taught Eden to swim. It was where everyone partied, got drunk and high, made love, and swam naked.

Scooter parked and shifted in the seat to face her. "Were you able to reach those two guys I told you about?"

She had called before hiking to the restaurant. The manager at the Ink It tattoo parlor said Jeff hadn't worked there in months. "And he didn't tell us where to send his weekly check from the lottery," the manager had said. Eden got similar results when she called the fish market to ask about Hank.

"Nope. And there is no word as to where they are," Eden said.

He tipped the cowboy hat away from his face. "I apologize. I'll make some more calls for you, see what else I can come up with." His smile flashed.

"Thanks," she said.

"So did Meg invite you anywhere?"

A quiet like a mound of wet sand settled between them as Eden considered the question.

"She did."

"Watch out."

Eden stared beyond the window, ignoring the comment. A couple of surfers were riding into shore. Red Parker's Reef was located on the horizon east of the old pier. She thought of wrecks waiting at the bottom of the dark sea. They waited for her. Her hands began to sweat.

"We're going diving," Eden said.

"Where to?"

"The reef."

Scooter shook his head. "Unless you're a Navy Seal, I wouldn't do it. You might not get out of there alive."

"I could say the same about riding in this car with you. But gosh, thanks for being so concerned about me. By the way, Meg had good things to say about how your sister is this successful businesswoman. She said Kathy was one of Jess's friends."

Scooter hadn't mentioned Kathy, Jess's friendship with her, or with Meg. On the other hand, he had given her the names of two guys she hadn't been able to locate. Scooter nodded as if acknowledging Eden had scored points because of her obvious awareness of his omissions and intentional misdirection meant to discourage her.

He had been happy to cast suspicion on Johnny while professing him a good guy, and he had tried to keep her from talking to others who might have some useful information. But then again, neither Johnny nor Aunt Billie had been encouraging about finding Jess, and she decided they all knew something they weren't about to share. She wondered what else the game with Scooter would produce. She didn't have to wait long.

Scooter reached into the backseat. He opened the lid of a small cooler, extracting two cans of beer, handing her one. He set the other between his legs. He rummaged inside a well in the vehicle door and removed a hand-rolled cigarette, set a match to it. A long drag, the pungent smoke familiar to her.

He sat smiling to himself. She had no problem with dope. But she did have an immediate problem with the coffee from the marina, which was too much with her. She opened the door and slid out.

Scooter called after her, "What's up? I offend you or something?"

"I'm needing fresh air."

Behind her, a Magnolia Beach patrol car pulled into the clearing. It slowed near Scooter's car, the policewoman giving her a long stare before letting her gaze wander over other vehicles parked there. The patrol car moved on toward the main road. Eden stood on the walkway steps. She watched the patrol car leave the clearing. Then she looked out to sea.

She and Jess had come often to this place. She spoke to her in silence, telling her she would find her. As if in answer, she felt the wind touch her face and hair. She returned to the vehicle and climbed in. Scooter was turning over a straight-blade knife, holding it up to examine.

"Survival knife," Eden said. "Is it any good?"

"Thinking of trading it for something better," he said. He looked at her over the blade edge before setting the knife in the well of the door. "You okay?"

"Yeah."

"Even when you didn't feel so hot, you looked pretty. You ever thought of modeling?"

Eden glanced at her torn stained jeans, her faded running shoes. He had probably said the same things to Jess to try to involve her in his little picture business.

"It's the first thing I think about at 4 a.m. when I'm escorting the cockroaches out of the diner where I work. They take over at night."

She straightened her shoulders, trying to ward off a deepening sense of discomfort. It wasn't the pot. It was everywhere and rapidly being legalized, which made sense to her. One day, once they got the regulations worked out so they were manageable and the illegal markets had faded, it would bring in tax revenues. It wasn't weed and it wasn't the knife. Summers with Luke, Johnny, and

Jess, she'd learned to use one. And it wasn't the compliments, either, although they usually came with someone wanting a piece of her in return. She could handle it.

Most likely it was the combination of things, along with being in this place, remembering Jess but not being able to see her or hear her voice. Missing her with an ache the way she imagined phantom pain might feel in the stump of a severed limb.

He drove her to the lodge. Since talking with him at the downtown commercial pier, she'd puzzled over the color of his eyes. As she stepped from his car onto the lodge driveway, she glanced across her shoulder. He was staring at her. His eyes were the color of water in the bottom of a boat.

***

Back in her room at the lodge, she visited Scooter's website. After studying pictures of fresh caught large dead fish, she moved on to a description of his business and views of his boat taken from different angles. There were a few customer reviews but not nearly as many as she had expected:

"Could've been a longer trip for the money, but great time had by all!!"

"It didn't seem like he was prepared to provide enough snacks and sandwiches or beer but still a fun day trip!"

Scooter appeared to run a legitimate business, but it could do double duty as a cover for drug trafficking.

She moved on to check Twitter, Instagram, and Jess's Facebook page, as she did several times a week in the remote hope she'd posted. There were pictures from before she'd vanished, of underwater worlds, fantasy pictures of mermaids, photos of foxes, and quotes from famous authors. From Shakespeare's *The Tempest*: "We are such stuff as dreams are made on; and our little life is rounded with a sleep."

Among her last entries was a passage by Anne Morrow Lindbergh. Eden read it again, liking it more each time: "And when we are tired of walking, we lie flat on the sand under a bowl of stars. We feel stretched, expanded to take in their compass. They pour into us until we are filled with stars, up to the brim." Eden wondered who the "we" might have been for Jess at the time she wrote the entry. Johnny didn't have a reputation as a stargazer.

She looked at a few other sites, but there were no postings she could identify as coming from Jess. And Jess wasn't into false identities. Eden went back to Facebook feeling like she was failing to consider something about her cousin she already knew, and this meant she might have overlooked a path she ought to follow in her search. Each time she thought she could give it a name, it danced into the shadows out of reach.

Eden slipped her phone into her pocket. She had hoped for something signaling Jess was still alive.

It wasn't going to happen.

Chapter Nine

Eden didn't have anything against dimly lit chandeliers and scented candles, or even the way the woman behind the desk kept her eyes focused on a place somewhere past her shoulder, as if Eden didn't exist. She assumed the glance excluding her meant the Salon & Spa Elegance was maintaining the highest standards of classiness, and she didn't fit in, her jeans neither torn nor faded enough to make a fashion statement, her haircut self-inflicted. Still, something bothered her about the place other than the windowless room and how she was being treated. She couldn't put a finger on it.

"We're booked solid here, sweetie," the woman behind the desk was saying with a *leave-before-I-call-the-cops* gleam in her eyes. "You need to go somewhere you can get in right away. Hold on, let me see what I can find."

She came out from behind the desk and started tapping something into her phone as she walked briskly toward the door, Eden getting the message

71

she was supposed to meekly follow. And keep going. Instead she hung back and watched.

The woman she'd come there to see, the woman with the phone, was heavier than she remembered, and the patterned silk top with plunging neckline, flowing sleeves and matching pants were a world away from the fanny-sculpting cut-offs she used to show up in at dunes parties. Dark hair highlighted with green and tied in a ponytail swung from one side of her head. The other side was shaved. Her nails and lips were a red so deep it looked black. Like old blood.

Kathy read from the list produced on her phone. "Most of these places should be within walking distance, sweetie. In fact, one's about a mile across the highway in an old shopping center, the one with boarded windows? I'm sure there's a way to get over there from here on foot. Be careful of the traffic, sweetheart." As if Eden was a four-year-old.

Eden reached for a business card from a plastic holder and pushed it into a pocket of her jeans. "I'll take a look at my schedule and call you later for an appointment," she said, enjoying Kathy's startled look.

"Of course, sweetheart."

In these parts nearly everyone flung around "honey," or "darling," or "sweetie." Sometimes this felt like a warmhearted verbal hug reaching out to bring a stranger into the family. Eden didn't think this was the intent here, coming from Kathy as it did with a smirk.

It was more like a subtle form of control as in, "I will refer to you as 'sweetie' and you won't object to it like you would a glass of sweet tea dumped on your head although it's about the same thing, because I've got power, and money, so I can and will call you whatever cutesy little thing I want."

Her friend from the Blue Moon Trailer Park, Kitty, called her "honey" which was fine, because Eden could hear the love in it. But for Eden to call someone sweetie would be the equivalent of stuffing gum down her windpipe. She stared at Kathy and gave her the message she'd gone there to deliver. "At some point, Kathy, I hope you and I can get together and talk over coffee."

"And what would we talk about?" She had returned from the door to the reception desk.

"Jess Sinclair. I'm her cousin, Eden."

Kathy grew suddenly interested in the hair products lined up on a shelf to one side of and above the desk. She fiddled with the bottles and jars before facing Eden.

"She was one of my dearest friends. So sad." She forced a tight smile. "I remember my brother mentioning you were staying at the lodge. Working as a housekeeper. I heard they can't get help. Lousy pay, but it must not be too bad since you are willing to work there. It is such a shame the way it's gone downhill. Do you see much of Johnny?"

Her fake eyelashes fluttering, the smile shifted into high gear, but the important question on Kathy's mind had been left unasked: was Eden sleeping with Johnny? Kathy wasn't good at disguising her feelings, at least not about Johnny.

"He's around the lodge for a few hours every day."

Kathy studied her nails. "Poor Johnny always needs a meal and a clean shirt. We love him, though. Tell the poor guy to come in any time for his monthly haircut. It's something I do for charity."

Kathy had spoken of Johnny like he was a child in need of a handout. It was a rhetorical tactic Eden had learned about in school called "poisoning the well." In this case it was being used to make her find Johnny undesirable. Eden had her emotional ups and downs about Johnny, but he was her childhood fantasy sweetheart, and she wasn't going to turn from him because of something Kathy said. Or the rumors.

"I expect he'll be over for dinner tonight. I'll tell him you want to see him. And I'll call you later for an appointment."

Eden walked to the door. Whether Jess was alive or dead didn't matter to Kathy. Kathy's face glowed even when she was putting Johnny down, and her ridiculous false lashes didn't conceal how her eyes went all liquid and dark when she spoke his name.

Eden wondered to what lengths Kathy might've gone in order to make Johnny hers when beautiful Jess had still been around to dance with him at the dunes.

She stood on the steamy pavement, relieved to be outside again and away from the spa's cold perfection. It had felt lifeless in there except for Kathy's desire for Johnny.

Eden understood her desire.

She stepped outside and turned her face to the rain.

Chapter Ten

They waited in a treeless yard surrounded by a wire fence. They waited for food. For a shower. For something to keep them going for another day or a few hours. Eden was certain this was the shelter Meg had told her about. But there was no identifying sign other than the evidence of human need. She walked over to a young man who was inspecting a bicycle. Eden asked him if this was Harbor Place.

"Yes, ma'am," he said with a gentle smile, and she saw there was a cut beneath his eye. He wheeled the bike from the yard and went on down the road.

A girl about Eden's age sat on the steps leading into a small building. She glanced at Eden and shifted a backpack to one side to make room for her.

The skin was flaking off her nose and cheeks. Eden recognized the sign of too much sun. She walked over and sat on the step below the girl. The girl reached into her backpack and produced a bag of chips, opened the sealed bag, and offered them to Eden. She took one. And Eden remembered her as the girl she'd sat next to on the Greyhound bus from Chicago to Florida. The girl had shared her chips then, too.

Eden and the girl had mostly slept and kept to themselves during the long bus ride. On the steps at Harbor Place, Eden learned the girl's name was Wanda. She had left Chicago behind to meet her boyfriend and start a new life.

She was eager to talk. "He swore this place has weather like paradise. You ask me, he must never have been here before and once he did get here he never set foot outside because it's nothing but pouring rain followed by wet heat steaming a person like a sorry vegetable, mosquitoes and cockroaches running around like they own the place, which you could argue they do."

Eden described the town west of Chicago where she'd lived with Annie and for a few months with Ted. Wanda said she knew the place having been there to visit her brother when he worked in food service at the university.

"What brings you here?" she asked.

"To Harbor Place or Florida?"

"Both."

She hadn't gone beyond small talk during the bus trip, but Eden had been friendly to the extent of helping Wanda out of her sweater, even neatening it some before handing it over. Mostly she'd slept or watched the eighteen-wheelers sliding by.

Eden felt more like talking with Wanda. She told her about Jess disappearing from the lodge. "I have a job at my aunt's place. I'm going to find out what's become of my cousin."

"It's the guys. They are usually the ones who cause all the heartache and trouble, the one a woman's closest to," Wanda said. "Or wanted to be able to depend on." Wanda's shoulders lifted and fell with a despairing sigh.

"It's too often the truth," Eden said. She remembered her last glimpse of Wanda at the end of the trip when they were inside the bus depot. Wanda had taken a seat near the door and fixed her eyes on it, her hands clutched tight in her lap, willing her boyfriend to appear and sweep her into his arms.

"Did your friend ever come for you at the depot?"

"No. I wound up hitching a ride. Can't believe I took such a chance, but it worked out." She shrugged. Eden had done the same and nodded agreement. It wasn't a preferred way of getting around.

"Anyway, he showed up here later, and I got to spend some time with him before he took off for Miami. He says he'll call me once he's gotten a job and a place for us to live. Meanwhile, I'm here and looking to get work of my own. He's my fiancé." Wanda was not wearing a ring, but then neither was Eden. Ted said he'd get her one as soon as they'd paid off some of their debt mostly for Ted's clothes and hobbies.

Wanda clasped her hands between her knees and stared at the drifting sand creeping over the road's edge beyond the fence. A car sped by. The sand whirled.

She sat up straight and faced Eden. "If you give me your number, I'll call if I hear anything about your cousin. I'll ask around."

Eden was thinking if she gave Wanda her number, she might become a pest. Wanda turned her head from Eden and crunched on a chip.

"I don't have a phone," Wanda said in a near whisper. Eden decided Wanda was trying to assure her she wouldn't ask for anything. Like friendship. Eden wrote out her name and number and her cousin's name on a slip of paper and handed it to Wanda.

The sky darkened, and she got up off the step and left Harbor Place. She walked past burned lawns and businesses constructed of cinderblocks and apartments with damp laundry hanging outside to dry. The palms, loaded with brown boughs, were half-alive. She walked toward the beach.

The sea had turned a deep green under the gray sky. Over at the commercial pier fishermen were stowing their gear and hurrying with wheeled coolers and carts toward the parking lot. A grassy strip wide enough for benches under a row of palms bordered the lot. A young teen on one of the benches rocked forward and back like a mother soothing a crying child. Her cradling arms were empty.

Eden wondered what hurt she was holding on to. She sat next to her on the bench and introduced herself. She felt awkward beside the girl, like she might be thought to be prying, and she didn't want to be thought of in this way. Eden told her about Harbor Place where she could get food and a shower and meet people. There was even a medical clinic, Eden said, and job counseling.

"Yeah," the girl said. Eden had trouble hearing her, the girl's voice was so thin and high, a piece of cloth fluttering in an attic's busted window. It was as if there was nobody home where the voice came from.

"Can I make a call for you or help somehow?" she asked.

The girl shook her head. After a moment, Eden stood up and walked away. Before she was out of viewing range, she glanced across her shoulder.

A guy with long greasy hair had propped his booted foot against the girl's thigh. He leaned forward over her legs, removed a lit cigarette from between his lips, and held it out to her. She took it, inhaled, handed it back. He helped her up by the elbow. They walked away, him giving her a hard slap on the rear before clamping his hand possessively on her hip. Sex, money, and cruelty. The combination never went out of style.

Eden wanted to run and catch him somewhere between the flashing signs for burgers and beer and twist his neck until his eyes bulged from his skull. His world of deadly drugs and sex might have hooked Jess, too. It was possible, even though the Jess she knew loved antique clothes and books with paper pages, pictures on her walls, and talking with people while sitting out on the porch with them after supper when her chores were done. She liked to listen to guests' life stories. She loved dancing at the dunes. And exploring the ocean.

It was late afternoon as Eden walked to the lodge. The day was weighed down with clouds rumbling like freight trains from out of the west. Soon enough the train of clouds derailed and spilled its cargo of water. Eden sensed a figure moving across the dunes inside the gray curtains of rain, the figure pointing out to sea.

Chapter Eleven

Huge saucer eyes, a scrawny neck, and dirigible torso. Eden turned from the freaky funhouse reflection. It wasn't her true image, but she felt as though it might be. She walked across the room to her grandfather's narrow metal-frame bed. The quilt covering CJ's bed gave off puffs of dust as she sat on it. She thought about him. How her grandfather would never wear anything more formal than jeans or overalls. How he was a perfectionist, taking months to hand carve the wooden boxes he liked to make. Given his disinterest in appearance and his perfectionism, Eden wondered why CJ had gone to the trouble of attaching to his bedroom wall a warped full-length mirror.

She remembered the day he'd been working on its installation. It was the same day she and Jess stumbled upon a hidden compartment in the bedroom they shared at the lodge, and they had rushed to CJ's cabin to tell him of their find. He had built the lodge, and they were clever enough to have discovered the hiding place. They thought he would be pleased.

He'd set aside his tools. "If I ever hear one of you has gone and spilled the beans about what you uncovered, I'll give a severe thrashing to the both of you." Eden remembered Jess had laughed at the threat. He adored his granddaughters, though he loved Jess most of all.

They'd discovered the compartment by accident while moving a small cabinet in the closet holding both their clothes. Eden thought about secrets and her grandfather as she looked over at the mirror. Given CJ's personality and interests, it was beginning to make sense to her, this mirror. It could conceal more than it revealed.

She'd need help figuring it out. The lodge had internet access, and she pulled out her phone hoping to visit some useful sites. The phone had gone dead. Again. This had happened a few weeks ago.

She looked from the mirror toward the bedroom door. It was the wind finding its way between the cabin's wooden timbers causing those creaking sounds. The sound stopped, and she returned her attention to the phone.

She pushed and released several buttons simultaneously, then selected from among far too many unexplained and potentially disastrous restart options. It took some doing, but she got it working once more. To successfully restart twice she figured meant she could put off buying a new phone until she could afford it.

Eden's internet search disclosed many people with a desire for hiding places so intense they'd spent countless hours and dollars designing and building them. What they hid was stuff like guns, jewelry, and money. Probably drugs. Mostly it was ordinary stuff, nothing half so priceless as rare old books or love letters. And then there was the question why, after going to the work of building hidden places, people would then broadcast in brilliant meticulous detail all their smart construction secrets. But since so many had done this, she was eager to try out a few ideas.

She got up from the bed. In a few short steps she walked to the mirror and began probing its surface and frame. Nothing yielded, and she began working in combinations of moves. She was astonished when the mirror pivoted inward, revealing a walk-in storage compartment with a spider hanging from a cobweb in a corner. A sealed book carton sat on the floor.

Eden knelt and pulled off the tape holding the carton's flaps together. It was possible she'd find her grandfather's war medals somewhere inside the loose collection of torn and wadded papers the carton held.

She began to examine the papers. Pages were torn. Some were in shreds. She searched for an explanation of what she was looking at. No explanatory document surfaced.

CJ hiding a box of papers didn't mean they were important. And he might've put some in one place and others related to these in another. Or it could be they weren't his, and he hadn't been the one who'd stashed them.

She hadn't made much progress searching in the box or figuring out what she'd stumbled on when something about the cabin's atmosphere changed. It was as though the air had become crowded. There was a creaking sound again. It was coming from the hallway.

She looked around. There was nothing she could use for self-defense. Since her phone might act up, she had left a note on the kitchen table telling Ruth she'd be cleaning at CJ's for the afternoon. At least Ruth would have some idea where to begin looking for her if she hadn't returned in time to help prepare dinner. She got up off the floor. The spider's legs were disappearing in a crack in the wall as she closed the box and set the mirror door in place. She crossed the room.

"Hello?" she called. "Anyone here?" Eden moved swiftly along the hall toward the light washing in from the partly open front door. She could have sworn she had closed it behind her when she'd first entered the cabin, but it was possible she hadn't pushed hard enough for it to have stayed shut. She stepped onto the screen porch. The wilderness was heavy with damp heat. Rain was on the way.

"Eddie!" The shout came to her from a van parked near the kitchen. Johnny waved to her from the driver's side, and she walked down CJ's porch steps and along the path to the vehicle. He opened its door.

Johnny hardly waited for her to climb in before putting his arms around her, his lips seeking hers. "I've been thinking about you. About us," he murmured. "We should always be together," he said.

She'd imagined hearing words like these from him ever since she was a girl. And yet she found herself once again drawing away from him, reluctant even to meet his gaze. "I've been thinking about us, too," she said, her voice faint as the trace of rain in the air.

His hand slowly brushed a strand of hair from her neck. She raised her eyes to his, catching sight of his smile. "Something troubling you, Eddie? Don't try to hide it from me."

"I'm still married," Eden said, her voice small. She told herself this had to be the reason why she was feeling like the two of them being together still wasn't right. "Separated but not divorced."

Johnny shook his head. "There's a paper in a court somewhere, but you aren't married, Eddie, not feeling toward me the way you do and always have. I can see it in how you look at me. A woman can't pretend about love. She can't ever hide it, so don't even try."

Johnny's hands cupped her face, and she breathed in his scent of the wilderness, a deep hunger running through her veins. But there was something else, and it had her glancing through the windshield.

"What is it?" Johnny asked.

"Nothing," she said. But it wasn't true. She had seen Jess's ghostly image inside the gathering gray of the coming rain. She was standing with her back to Eden, her arm extended as she pointed to the sea. A fox leaned against her. Eden longed for Jess and the fox to come to her.

"Listen, Johnny, there's something we need to talk about." He pressed a finger to her mouth, not letting her continue. His sea-green eyes moved over her face.

"You feel like she's coming home, but there's nobody but you believes after all this time it's going to happen. And you feel like her and me belong to each other so therefore you should keep a distance between us. Eddie, listen to me. You need to let her go so you can get on with your life, and we can have something together. Someday you and me, we'll find a place away from here. I'd like to go into the mountains. We'll have a big double bed with a thick quilt on it. I'll take care of you, Eddie, like I did when you were drowning. You were dying, and I held onto you, I saved you. Remember?"

"I won't ever forget," she said. She stared through the windshield at the blank gray sky. She no longer saw Jess and the fox.

He pushed his fingers through her hair, and she felt her body yielding to him. His hands slid along her upper arms. For several heartbeats she believed in what he'd said about needing to let Jess go so she could live a life with him. Hadn't she dreamed of the day when she and Johnny would be together? She'd dreamed it, and the months went by, and Jess did not return. Eden and Johnny hadn't spoken, though, and gradually she'd sent him into another room inside herself and closed the door. She'd gone off and married someone else. She didn't understand how she could've done this.

"Yes," she whispered. "A patchwork quilt."

Jess hadn't wanted Johnny anymore. Wasn't this so? They had broken up or they were about to. This was the way it had been. Eden would never have allowed what happened between her and

Johnny otherwise. Never. She told herself this was the truth.

It had begun to rain when the ugly rumors started to scald her, and a voice inside her ordered, "Ask him, Eden."

"She's dead. What happened and where is she? I need to find out before I can move on. You're not being straight with me, Johnny."

He set his hands together as if they were bound with handcuffs, and he balanced them on the top of the steering wheel and gave her a sideways glance. His eyes were shadowed like a winter sea.

His voice low and dark, he said, "You're asking because of what people are saying about how I killed Jess over losing a home at the lodge and ownership of it one day." He shook his head in wonderment, the gesture showing he believed they were wrong.

He stared at the streaks of rain on the windshield. "Did I murder her like they whisper? It's your question, isn't it? It hurts, Eddie, knowing you would even think it because the answer is in your heart."

There was a tapping sound on the passenger window. Her long blond-gray hair spread on her shoulders, Aunt Billie grinned up at her from under an umbrella. Eden, feeling like the rain was falling inside of her skin, feeling unsure of Johnny, troubled by her doubts and wanting to get away, opened the door and jumped down.

The Camry had been fixed, and there was a new nightspot in town, but Aunt Billie didn't want to drive herself there. Would Eden meet her after dinner and take her downtown? Eden agreed, and Johnny said, "C'mon, Miss Billie, I'll give you a lift across the road." The rain was coming down with less space between the drops.

She knew Johnny was unhappy with her. She couldn't worry about it, she had work to do, and so she started along the forest path to CJ's place. This time she opened the mirror door with ease and looked in at the box of papers. The rain was coming down and the box was flimsy. She took a handful of papers from the box, and closed the mirror door. Eden ran to the lodge, the papers making the trip stuffed under her shirt.

Upstairs, she dragged the three-drawer storage cabinet from the corner of Jess's closet, then pulled on a wooden tab. A cover lifted off, and there was the compartment Jess and Eden had rushed to tell CJ about years ago.

It was wide and deep. But crude, the lid arrangement not at all sophisticated like the ones she'd seen on the internet. Folded advertising pages torn from a newspaper provided a protective lining, but there would be room enough to hold all

CJ's papers when she had time to retrieve and return with the remaining ones.

Downstairs in the kitchen, Ruth said, "Good thing I got the message you left or I would've sent for the police if you hadn't shown up pretty soon. I need you to grab a knife and do some slicing for tonight. Something came for you in the mail. It's over on the table."

The unsigned note had been mailed at the local post office. There was no return address. It had been constructed from words and letters cut from magazines: "I see you through the window and in my dreams. I am full of longing for you. One day you will see me, too."

The message was creepy. She felt violated, and she slipped it into her pocket and walked to the sink and washed her hands. She stared at the lettuce and tomatoes.

"Everything all right?" Ruth asked.

Eden thought it over but decided it was best not to worry her. There wasn't a thing Ruth could do about it after all.

"Yes," she said, as she began to chop vegetables for the salad, her thoughts stuck on the uncomfortable realization the person who'd sent the awful note was probably someone she knew.

Chapter Twelve

Eden followed Aunt Billie into the hallway at her cottage and down the stairs to the car parked in the garage below. Less than ten minutes later they were stalled in the beach community's downtown traffic. Crowds were drawn there by restaurants and shops Eden couldn't afford, and bars where she was old enough to fix and serve drinks but couldn't consume legally. Aunt Billie directed her to stop in front of a brick building where a line was forming. It was Saturday night.

Her aunt reached into the glove compartment. She removed the little perfume atomizer and gave herself a couple of squirts. The scent of stale air freshener in an unwashed public restroom wafted through the car.

"You want some?" she asked.

"It just isn't me, Aunt Billie," Eden said.

"If you change your mind, it will be right here."

"Yes, ma'am. I won't forget."

Aunt Billie set the atomizer in the glove compartment. There was a muffled clunky sound of something heavy being moved around inside.

Eden thought she might be about to pull out the Ladysmith revolver, and she wondered what, if anything, she ought to say in the event this happened. Which it did.

"If you ever need a gun, there's one right here. You probably found it already." Aunt Billie waggled the gun at Eden.

Eden said, "Is it loaded?"

"Cap gave it to me for my birthday," Aunt Billie said, ignoring the question as she returned the weapon to the glove compartment. "He can be such a wonderful guy when he wants. I mean, what a sweet gift."

"So romantic," Eden said.

Aunt Billie didn't pause. "It's why I'll take him back, same as before."

She opened the car door. "You can go on to the lodge. I won't be needing a ride home." She winked at Eden and waved.

This information answered Eden's unspoken question as to whether her aunt would invite her along. She was thinking about finding parking and going in anyway when Cap called.

"I'm at the cabin a while longer. You can come on over." She knew she was taking a chance going to his place alone at night, but it would be an opportunity to question him about Jess and hear what he had to say.

He met her at the top of his porch steps with a hug. It lasted too long. Inside, he moved a stack of magazines off a chair at the dining room table and she sat down, Cap drawing up a chair for himself and sitting across from her.

Mail and brochures were piled on the table beside a television and the old typewriter she and Jess used to practice on. His hunting trophies were mounted behind him on the wall: shark and alligator jaws, antlers, a sea turtle shell, a fox. Their wildness and beauty would never die.

Even with the clutter on the table, there was an unlived-in feeling about the place. She asked if he was moving out.

"Taking my time," he said. "How are things going with the housekeeping and kitchen duties?"

"There's a lot of work to be done, sir," she said.

She and Jess used to go with their grandfather, with Cap driving his vintage Chevy, to the downtown DQ for ice cream, also fishing with Cap and CJ. There had been some good times, and she thought it might be helpful in talking with him if she kept this history in mind.

But it was difficult to remember the good moments when she caught him staring at her the way he was.

Cap folded his arms across his chest and stretched his legs before him. His usually flushed face was a white blob in the dim light. There was a smell of spoiling food from fast-food containers at the far end of the table. Picnic coolers lined the wall.

"You want a drink?" he asked, using the heel of his palm to slick the silver hair above his ears.

"None for me, thanks."

He got up and walked to the back of his cabin and opened the big double-door refrigerator. He returned to his chair with two bottles of beer. "In case you change your mind," he said. He filled a glass from one of the bottles.

"I understand you've been looking for CJ's war medals over there." He nodded in the direction of her grandfather's cabin. The cabin was about two hundred feet to the north of his place.

"Yes, sir," she said. "They'll turn up."

"Your aunt wants you to come to me with whatever else you stumble on, too, like papers," he said, "so I can make sure we haven't missed paying his debts."

"Of course, sir."

"He liked to hide things. I'll try real hard to see what I can do to help you out, if you want. I have business interests keeping me tied up, but—" He let the sentence trail. Eden thought Cap didn't want to be bothered with a search at CJ's. Meanwhile, Aunt Billie was lazy and often hungover.

"I can manage," Eden said. She wasn't sure what was going on except it seemed as though they were sending her on a fishing expedition with the war medals as a pretext. Instead of telling him of her find, she decided she would continue to look at the papers she'd transferred to the lodge and go back for the others. She'd need to study them all more closely.

His eyes were moving over her, staying a long time on her mouth, continuing to rove. The buttons on her shirt were of particular interest.

She said, "Could a private investigator be hired to look for Jess?"

"Billie can't afford anything like a detective," he said, picking the dirt from under a fingernail. "Besides, there was a search party."

"Who was in it?" Someone interested enough in finding Jess would be worth talking to.

Cap shrugged and gazed in the direction of the porch. "People from around here, I'll need to refresh my memory," he said. He studied the backs of his hands.

"Any theories about what happened to her?" Eden asked.

He gulped the beer, set the glass down. "Listen," he said, "I have already been asked what became of her, and all I can say is she was a wildcat, impudent, in love with herself, and she had a way of enraging other folks. We don't have enough money to keep the lodge up much less spend a lot of time looking for Jess. We've got people depending on us here. Whereas Jess, she's run off, probably high all the time." He swallowed the remains of the beer.

Eden ignored this caricature of her cousin. Meg would've mentioned if drugs had been a problem for Jess.

He shifted in his chair and extracted his phone from a pocket of his jeans. He paused, listening, and from the other end of the phone the sound of laughter, booming music, and Aunt Billie's voice, her words indistinct, gushed into the cabin.

"It's all good," he said to Aunt Billie. Rising from the chair, he turned to Eden. "Listen, beautiful, I've got to get going."

He guided her toward the porch door with his hand tight on her upper arm. She pretended to stumble and broke his grip.

Cap rested with his back against the doorframe, but the glitter in his eyes told her he was far from relaxed. "One other thing. Don't burden your aunt with what you might turn up. She's had a tough time losing her son, daughter, and CJ." He paused. "And your mom."

"And Billie and Annie were so close," Eden said. Neither had communicated for most of their lives.

They crossed the porch, Cap handing her a flashlight so she could make her way through the dark forest. She hadn't gotten far when she heard footsteps behind her. She directed the flashlight beam onto the path.

It was Cap, his paunchy figure clad in camouflage swaggering toward her. He grabbed her by the arm, and before she could smash him in the teeth with the flashlight, he shoved her against a tree and kissed her, his heavy breath hot and putrid. She struggled to free herself as he rubbed himself against her.

A bullet ripped through the air, tunneling above his head into the tree bark. "What the f—," Cap screamed as he jumped back. More gunfire sent branches, leaves, and chunks of wood flying. Cap fled in the direction of the Chevy. She heard the engine turn over and saw its taillights disappear along the drive.

Eden had started jogging to the lodge when a series of splashes drew her attention to the lake. The sounds were probably from an alligator turning over from its stomach to its back in a death roll as it cracked bones, tore into meaty flesh. Cap belonged in there, swimming with the 'gators.

She began to jog faster to the lodge, its yellow lights shining behind twisted limbs hung with moss, when about fifty feet from the east side of the forest path and parallel to it there was rapid motion between the trees. She put on a burst of speed.

After passing the shed, she sensed whoever or whatever was out there had moved farther to the east, the sounds fading. Her phone buzzed. She shoved her hand in the pocket of her jeans and pressed its off button as she reached the south porch. She went inside.

A check of her phone identified the caller. Everything was going to work out between them after all. He had called because he'd missed the sound of her voice. She was still catching her breath when he answered her return call.

"So what's happening?"

"Someone or something was following me."

Ted gave a half-laugh. "A zombie or werewolf? How about a chainsaw murderer?"

"Don't you wish."

It might have been Cap. Again. But he would have attacked if he'd changed his mind and come after her one more time. It was something or someone else. Ted would blame her for Cap's behavior, so she didn't mention him. "You must have worn something to have excited him," Ted would say.

"Look, I'm calling because I wanted to see how you're getting along. And from what you've said, I'm thinking you'd better start taking your meds again, Eden, if you've stopped taking them, which is what it sounds like."

He did have a point, because she'd gotten the strangest sense about whatever had been shadowing her. It was keeping a benign eye on her. She wiped her sweaty hands on her jeans and imagined Ted saying he loved her. This, too, was irrational.

"Anyway," he said, "I wanted to say hello." He hadn't suggested Eden might call the police, he hadn't said he wanted her to come home, and he was certainly eager to stop talking with her.

He wasn't in the least worried about her. She suspected he'd called to find out if she was still alive. If Eden fell dead, he'd inherit the flat-screen TV. His calling was not a hopeful sign after all. She felt more alone than ever.

She felt beyond bitter.

"Well, so long then." Eden struggled to sound upbeat, but the signoff was bumpy, like there was a hangman's knot in her throat. She slipped the phone into her pocket and stumbled up the stairs to the second floor.

Standing in Jess's darkened room, she felt Cap's hands and mouth on her, heard again the music from the club, heard the gunshot and the sounds in the forest as she was being followed. And she heard Ted's uncaring voice. Everything about this summer night made her shiver with disgust and fear and loneliness.

She stood in the middle of Jess's room with her arms at her sides. She was in a cage. The cage of herself.

She wanted to run.

From the poster she'd helped Jess put on the wall, a fox gazed at her. Shadows flowed through the room, shifting shapes. A tree limb turned into a slender arm. The window was open and she could hear the wind whispering like a restless spirit.

Eden slept in Jess's bed, worked at her job, and met her friends, if she could call them friends. She walked over to the dresser and looked in its mirror. In the ghost-gray light, she saw Jess in her reflection. She resembled her more with each passing day.

A sound outside in the hall had her moving swiftly to the closed bedroom door. "Eddie?" His voice came to her in a whisper.

She let him in and closed the door, and when he took her in his arms, this time she did not resist. Outside in the moonlight, in the rising wind, a fox raced over the dunes to the sea.

Chapter Thirteen

Thunder rolled across the sky. Lightning flickered beyond a window, illuminating CJ's bed and the floor around it. The flickering light and the flashlight's powerful beam showed something emerging sideways from the gap between the edge of the quilt on his bed and the floor. Eden stepped back. The snake moved rapidly forward across the room. It didn't stop as it made its way into the hall. She followed at a distance.

A breath of warm moist air touched her skin. As she stepped into the kitchen, she saw the back door hanging open. An intruder had been in the cabin. He or she had fled from the snake or because of Eden's arrival on the scene.

She watched the snake wind its way over the threshold and vanish into the weeds growing up through the stairs. A light rain began to fall. Eden closed the door and returned to CJ's bedroom.

She'd gone back to CJ's cabin after Johnny had left her and she couldn't sleep. What she'd found— the mirror door to the hidden storage area gaping, the carton overturned—told her what she'd suspected: she'd been spied on earlier. Eden grabbed the remaining torn papers and returned to the lodge. Lights were on inside.

Ruth was seated at the kitchen table when Eden walked in.

"I thought I heard something. It must've been you." Ruth directed a sharp glance at Eden as she set her findings on the table and took a chair across from Ruth.

"What's all this?"

"Papers I came across at CJ's." She glanced through them quickly, confirming the contents were in the same tattered condition as what she'd already stored in the closet upstairs. "I left some of them behind from when I was there earlier. I couldn't sleep and I went back for the rest."

From the way Ruth was studying her, it was clear she wasn't satisfied she had heard the whole story of Eden's late-night trip to the cabin. She had to tell her something more. The best course was not to mention the theft or the snake. There was no point in worrying the elderly woman.

"I can't make any sense of the papers, but Cap wants me to give him stuff I find over there."

"Don't you give him anything," Ruth snapped. "What's in them?"

"Snatches of property descriptions, from what I've seen. There's no explanation for where the property is or what any of it's about. There are mostly torn pages."

Ruth leaned into her arms folded before her on the table. "It could be you've found something having to do with CJ's will."

"His will?"

"CJ had Jess hide it."

"There's no document with the court?"

"CJ kept his business dealings private. I do not believe he ever filed anything with the courts."

Eden got up and filled a glass with water from the tap. She drank it down and returned to the table. "Aunt Billie told me she owns the lodge."

"She told me the same thing after CJ died, but she'd have shown off the physical proof if she had any."

Upstairs in her room, Eden pulled out her phone and consulted several legal websites, thereby increasing her grasp of anything to do with wills by a hundred percent. Before long she'd learned a missing will was treated by the court as if there was no will, and the first person to inherit from someone dying without a will was the surviving spouse.

CJ's wife had divorced him years ago, a thing which had been of no surprise to anyone who knew CJ. Given the absence of a spouse, the next of kin would inherit.

Her thoughts turned to the people she could reach close to midnight who would give her a solid legal opinion as to what it all might mean. Her friend Kitty immediately came to mind. Kitty's ex-husband was a felon serving time in prison. This gave Kitty a certain authority in speaking on matters having to do with the law.

Kitty would read text messages, but she would never send one unless she had to. She preferred using the phone. This was understandable because her voice was all satin and smoke like a lounge singer from the fifties. She sent a text message to Kitty asking for her guidance.

Kitty's smoky voice came to her immediately. "How are you? Are things going well?"

"Yes. But here's the thing. Jess hid my grandfather's will. In the absence of a will, my aunt as next-of-kin gets the lodge. She and her boyfriend asked me to look for CJ's war medals, but I suspect what they want is for me to find the document. Why bother? Already she's claiming she's the owner."

"Honey, if there is a will, it will surface, and they know or suspect old CJ didn't leave the lodge to your aunt. They want to get their hands on the document before anyone else does. Then they'll doctor it to show your aunt *is* heir to his entire estate."

"They told me to turn over anything I found."

"They're counting on you being obedient and not being interested enough to read old legal papers. Definitely don't turn over even a receipt from the drycleaners." Kitty was silent. "Have you ever thought you could be one of your grandfather's heirs?"

"Annie told me he'd disinherited her for marrying my dad." She thought a moment. "Jess may have been the intended heir. And she's missing."

"You must keep your door locked at night," Kitty advised.

"Yes, ma'am," Eden said.

After the call ended, thoughts of CJ, Jess, Annie, and Luke swirled in her mind. The lost feeling of being unattached, of not belonging anywhere or with anyone came over her, and she got up off the floor and went to a corner of the room where she'd left her backpack. She thrust her hand in the bag, fishing around for what she knew was at the bottom. She grasped it and pried off the container's lid.

One bright-colored capsule would carry her for hours in a cushioned space free from the painful highs of panic and anxiety, where dread, grief, fear, and sadness would be leveled to a comfortable evenness. On the meds she felt numb, everything inside her flat as a tombstone.

But as shadows flowed around her, she realized she needed to allow fear and loneliness and anger into her bones. She should not send the feelings away like troublesome children. Because if she were ever to find Jess, she had to let in the currents of life at all levels of her being. Besides, if things got too awful, the meds were within reach.

She gathered the papers and went to the closet, pulling aside the three-drawer storage cabinet and uncovering the compartment in the floor. She set the papers in with the others. Eden returned the lid and moved the cabinet to its place. She shut the closet and fell across the bed, waking after midnight to sounds from the driveway.

A van's red taillights were disappearing around the corner of the east porch going south in the direction of the toolshed. Eden debated returning to bed, deciding instead to investigate. She moved silently down the stairs through the sleeping lodge to the darkened south porch.

Chapter Fourteen

A spotlight shone into the trees from Cap's place. The van was parked with its rear doors opening onto the cabin stairs, blocking a clear view. But Eden could make out two figures moving around inside the porch. One of them was Cap. The other man, in a cowboy hat, was Scooter.

They were in a hurry going in and out of the cabin, taking turns loading the van, but with the trees, angle of the van, and distance, she couldn't be sure exactly what was going into the back of the vehicle. From the few shapes and flashes of white she caught sight of, the objects of their activity appeared to be picnic coolers.

Doors slammed, and soon thereafter the van, followed by Cap on his Harley, rumbled past the shed. Eden drew back in the darkness of the south porch as their headlights cut in her direction. The convoy moved along the drive until it turned at the stone posts and headed north on the main road.

Drugs of every kind were easy to buy on the streets, at school, at parties.

Anywhere. She knew recovered addicts at the Blue Moon Trailer Park. There had been no obstacles for them to get all the help they needed to destroy their lives.

She wished she could be certain Cap and Scooter weren't using the lodge as their home base, but the activity she'd been witnessing together with what she already knew about Scooter suggested it was a strong possibility. Scooter and Cap were dealing.

If the two men were operating a business, Jess might have discovered it. Protecting a lucrative business offered a strong motive for them to have killed Jess if they thought she might turn them in.

Cap used to boast to her and Jess about killing the enemy in wars. Okay, the enemy had to die. Still, he boasted about killing human beings, and he had all those animal trophies on the wall. She didn't think he'd hesitate. And Scooter had made clear he was handy with a knife.

The two men could come back to the cabin at any time, but this was a risk she was willing to take if it meant she could find evidence of drugs beyond their casual use. She'd look for the other papers stolen from CJ's, too.

She'd started to open the south porch door, with the intent of walking through the forest to Cap's, when she heard something behind her moving inside the mostly darkened lodge. She

110

crossed the porch and gazed inside. A figure was emerging from the dining room. From the dim light cast by a small table lamp in a far corner, she could see a male figure in bathrobe and slippers.

"Good evening," Bobby Hayes said.

"Hi, Mr. Hayes. Is there something I can get you?"

"Thank you, I have what I came for," he said, holding up for her to see a large cookie wrapped in a napkin. He carried a glass of milk in the other hand. Guests knew there'd be milk and cookies available in the kitchen at bedtime in case they wanted a snack. It was a homey touch and she was glad to see Mr. Hayes enjoying this bit of comfort. His wife had died some years before. Eden watched as he moved along the hallway to his ground-floor bedroom.

She would check out Cap's cabin when the time was right. This might be a challenge since he came and went at odd times, and he hadn't asked her to do any cleaning over there. He and Scooter may have been doing nothing more than moving furniture.

Early the next morning, she heard the crunch of shells breaking on the driveway. From the east window she saw the same van from the night before making the turn toward Cap's. She walked down the stairs and crossed the common room to the south porch.

In the early morning light, she could see Cap and Scooter moving from the cabin to the back of the van. They were carrying a small sofa. She went inside with thoughts whispering to her of cocaine packed inside chair legs and stuffed in decorator cushions.

It was still early. Eden had some time before Ruth would expect her to help prepare and serve breakfast. She stepped into her swimsuit and headed to the beach.

A few surfers were already riding the waves. They rode like supermen. Until they jumped or fell into the pounding surf and stumbled out of the water, mortals again.

There was a guy out there spinning full circle on a short board. He was making those same moves he used to make while skateboarding. It was Johnny. There was a lull in the surf, and she ran along the edge of the waves, shouting his name to get his attention. He recognized her and gestured for her to swim out to him.

She told herself she could manage the strong surf. She could do it, she could reach him. If she was going to learn to surf, and if she was ever to go on an underwater dive with Meg, she had to get fear under control.

Eden dove through the waves, the ocean rising and falling the way her feelings did when she was around him, wanting him, doubting him, feeling guilty because Jess had loved him, and Eden wanted him. She told herself the talk of his murdering Jess was a malicious rumor. He'd saved Eden's life. It wasn't in him to take a life.

The moment she was in over her head, Eden found the current working against her and her strength ebbing fast. As she was swept away, she saw Johnny gazing toward the dunes. He wasn't looking for her. She tried to call to him.

Instead, she gulped a mouthful of water. A swell was building, its power and height increasing as it rolled toward her. It lifted her high, its tons of water like muscular arms holding onto her. She didn't struggle. She couldn't.

The wave carried her all the way to the beach and slammed her onto the sand. She pulled herself together and waited for Johnny.

"It wore you out," Johnny said when he emerged from the water and came over to sit with her. She wished his eyes weren't so filled with an expression somewhere in between concern and pity, when the other person is at ease and unafraid and feels you are not like them. She didn't want to see this in his eyes. She wanted Johnny to see her as being brave like Jess. It was a hard act to pull off with ropes of sand and seawater drooling down her cheeks and her hands trembling.

"I guess you didn't notice me out there?"

"You were in the water and the next thing I knew you were on the beach."

She was thinking of telling him it was a miracle for her to have made it to the beach alive. He should have kept his attention on her. The unspoken words bounced around inside her, silent to the human ear but making an awful emotional racket like something metallic rolling around in the bottom of a dumpster. For a moment she considered asking him for a surf lesson to show she was unafraid, but she decided she wouldn't. Not ever.

They hadn't gone surfing yet, but she thought she knew McCabe well enough to imagine when they did, if he saw her floundering around, he'd yell something bossy and she'd have to save herself so she could say something smart back.

Ted would tell her she was crazy.

Eden and Johnny fell silent, the wind drying them. Eden wondered what had been going on with him, where his thoughts were while she had struggled in the water. She stated one possibility. It was a way of asking again about Jess.

"Jess wants to be found."

He sat with his arms making a bridge across the tops of his knees. He looked out to sea toward Red Parker's Reef. "You got to think more about what you're doing by pursuing this," he said.

He grasped a handful of sand. "For our sake think about it, Eddie." Gazing at her, then glancing at the sand falling through his fingers. "But I'll do what I can." This time it was clear to Eden he thought finding answers was an impossible task, like counting all the grains of sand on the beach or even a few.

"What about drugs, Johnny? Could they have been involved in her disappearance?"

"Why? Have you found something?"

Eden shrugged.

Johnny shook his head. He squinted toward the horizon. "She didn't care about using. And she wouldn't snitch on anyone. She minded her own business."

Eden couldn't help but feel he was saying this for her benefit. She didn't care. She was not going to mind her own business where Jess was concerned.

"Did Jess ever say anything to you about CJ's will?"

"No." He jumped up and carried his board into the surf. He didn't look back.

Eden sat on the beach, the wind tasting of salt. Watching him stand at the edge of the waves, she felt like her heart was at the bottom of the sea. He didn't go in. Instead, still carrying his board, he came back and set it beside her.

"C'mon," he said, and he held out his hand to pull her up. "We belong together, Eddie. Bad weather or good." She took his hand, and they walked into the water. He kissed her wet shoulders, her neck. Her mouth. The waves broke around them.

Their bodies mingled like water, but she couldn't shake the feeling he knew what had become of Jess.

***

The envelope was propped on the kitchen table. It had been mailed from a nearby town. Her secret admirer had again constructed the note of words and letters clipped from the pages of newspapers and magazines. Eden took it upstairs to read.

"I want to kiss you. You will want me one day when you finally see me and know me. I will make sure this happens." The writer was becoming more intense, the prediction about the future especially troubling. Not for the first time Eden suspected it was a prank. She tossed the note in her wastebasket.

Chapter Fifteen

He took the board for a long ride into shore. Once he had reached shallow water he jumped off and walked up the beach. Eden watched him coming toward her, the board under his arm. He could probably eat a whole box of donuts without it ever showing on his lean and wiry frame. She had no excuse for not returning his text messages or calls. She looked around. There was no place to hide.

He propped the board in the sand and stared at her without smiling, but then smiling wasn't something she had ever seen him do. She hadn't been doing much of it either, or ever had.

Still, she wondered what his smile might look like. Was it crooked, wide, boyish, lopsided, rakish, or would it amount to no more than a hint of amusement? She didn't much care.

Eden figured he could reasonably anticipate at least an explanation from her as to why she had not responded to his messages. She decided a better approach would be to try to get him off balance so they could start the relationship on a fresh footing or end it right there.

"You still offering a free lesson, McCabe?"

"Lessons," he said.

The next day Eden was waiting when McCabe pulled up in the Silverado at the east porch. She felt pale and exposed even though she wore a shirt to hide the way Jess's tank suit clung to her in all the wrong places and was loose in others.

McCabe stared at her from behind aviator glasses as she walked down the sagging porch steps. He leaned across the seat to open the passenger door, Eden welcoming the scent of hot coffee as he poured two cups from a thermos, handing one to her when she was settled.

"You don't look like you'd want sugar or cream."

"A discerning observation, McCabe."

She grabbed a plump chocolate donut from the open box sitting between them and ate it quickly. McCabe guided the pickup along the drive beneath old leaning trees, making a left at the stone posts and moving north along the main road.

Two surfboards were stashed on pads in the bed of the pickup. McCabe was a careful driver, but he was making sure the boards wouldn't slide and bump around and get damaged on the trip. They reached the clearing near the walkway and big dune. Eden looked around while McCabe unloaded the boards.

The clearing of packed sand was crowded with vehicles. Eden searched the faces of the guys pulling boards from their trucks and vans, doors slamming, the low murmur of talk and laughter floating with the light streaming through overhanging trees tangled with moss and vines.

Guys with muscled tanned bodies and rings in their earlobes, tattoos covering their torsos, backs, arms, and legs, short guys, and tall guys, all of them carried boards along the wooden planks of the walkway toward the sea. There were no girls surfing today. They had to work; they were taking care of little kids. Or illness kept them out of the water. In any case, she was determined to stand tall for all the women who might have wanted to be there but could not make it.

She would surf every day if she could manage to get a feel for it and stay upright. Jess had learned, and so could she. She reminded herself she had reached the shore on her own after Johnny had forgotten she existed. She had been far offshore and had overcome some of her fears. Still, plenty remained. She needed to get them under control for diving if Meg called.

McCabe offered to carry her board. It was unwieldy, and she was tempted to hand it over, but pride would not let her. And so she trudged along, managing this first stage of the process with several stops and awkward adjustments. McCabe was ahead of her and, she hoped, unaware of her problems. Along the way Eden decided if she couldn't carry a board, she probably shouldn't be riding one.

She followed the walkway above the shallow valley carpeted with yellow and red flowers. Beyond the valley the walkway led over low shore dunes covered with clumps of sea oats bending in the wind. She took a flight of steps to the beach, and rested at the foot of its stairs. In the ocean's dancing lights, she pictured Jess with outstretched arms coaxing her to jump from the old pier. It reminded Eden of a child's drawing, the way the pier's spindly pilings wobbled into the ocean.

A surfer with a patchy beard and a lot of unruly hair gave Eden a long stare. She speculated about him. Of course he had surfed with Jess, and he had killed her. On a day like this, only death could keep her cousin from the ocean. Eden returned his stare. He nodded and smiled and trotted into the sea.

McCabe waited on the beach with his hands on his hips, unsmiling as usual, and she figured he was about to be the tough drill sergeant, punctuating critical remarks with arrogant displays of prowess as she attempted in her klutzy way to follow his barked directions.

This did not happen. Instead, he delivered pre-surfing instructions in a straightforward manner. Eden absorbed what he said, and soon she was practicing something McCabe called pop-ups.

These involved moving with lightning speed from face down on her stomach to kneeling, then standing fully upright on the board, ready for the power of a wave to carry her triumphantly to shore.

He estimated it would take ten minutes for her to get the hang of pop-ups. Well before then, she was drenched in sweat, her skin baking in the relentless sun. The three donuts she had eaten were like rocks in her gut.

Too soon she was in the water, her arms aching as she pulled against the current, following McCabe. By the time she began to fear McCabe was leading her into the shipping lane to be plowed under by a tanker, he turned his board so it faced the shore.

She reached his side and did as he had done. She had never been this far from the beach, and she wondered how long her false sense of security would last from having the board beneath her and McCabe at her side. She estimated Red Parker's was a few miles as the crow flies beyond where she was. This was a warm-up for nerving herself to go there. And then down beneath the waves.

But not this trip. Today was for surfing.

Her pale feet at the end of skinny legs dangled in the water like bait. She had seen the movie *Jaws* and several television specials on sharks. She'd seen news reports of attacks in California, Florida, and Massachusetts. She had also seen reports of shark hunts, and they sickened her. Of course sharks were all around, searching for food. It had been her choice to be where she was.

The sharks had not invited her, and she hadn't seen any. Instead, she saw Jess's face staring up at her from beneath the smooth surface of the water. In the reflection Eden recognized her cousin's determination. Once she had made up her mind to do something, Jess did it. She wondered if this might have been what had gotten her cousin into trouble, an unwise decision to do something, go somewhere, meet someone. Go into the water at night on a dare? She had done it. Run off for a few hours? Sure. But she would not run away for good. She loved this place too much.

McCabe told her to get ready. Coming up behind them was a giant swell. Eden flattened herself on the board. McCabe gave it a forceful push. She shot forward with the board miraculously still beneath her, catching the swell and paddling furiously to stay with the powerful tons of water speeding forward.

She popped up like he had taught her, and she was riding high. Eden had heard it described as a wall of water, and she thought it was a good description, except to her the wave was more like a horse galloping toward shore, or a dragon flying along. It was glorious.

For about half a second.

She toppled into the ocean, went down, and came up coughing but unharmed, grabbed the board and climbed on again, more paddling out, waiting, catching a wave, popping up and attempting to stand.

Falling.

Eden dragged her board from the water and collapsed on the sand. She stared at the oncoming surf and pictured Jess flying over the waves. Eden would try harder. She would do better. For Jess.

She was exhausted, but she was no longer afraid.

McCabe came out of the surf, his board balanced on his hip. With his free hand he brushed his hair forward over his brow, water streaming along the muscles of his body. He walked up the beach and stood in front of Eden.

"Learning to surf will take time and persistence, Eden. You'll need frequent practice if you aim for mastery. Anything less is unthinkable." Finger wagging was the one thing absent from this irritating lecture.

Without comment, Eden got up off the sand. She didn't feel like talking with him, so she started toward the clearing and his pickup, hauling the board with her. She felt his eyes on her. On the walkway she stopped at a shower to rinse the salt and sand from her body and the board.

Ahead, a dark-haired man with his shirtsleeves rolled up peered south through a pair of field glasses. The broad back and armpits of his shirt were wet with sweat. A suit jacket was draped next to him on the railing. A man with a snub-nosed profile stood beside him.

The man in shirtsleeves offered his companion the field glasses, but the snub-nosed man held out his phone so the other man could see it. The snub-nosed man jabbed a finger at it.

Eden finished her shower and continued along the walkway. Drawing near the men, she heard their raised voices. The dark-haired man snatched his jacket from the railing and the two men walked to the clearing.

The man with the jacket flung it over his shoulder and climbed in the back of a sedan. Doors slammed, and they drove off, the snub-nosed man at the wheel. Eden was close enough to see it was a black sedan with purple-tinted windows and a Miami license plate. She had seen the car before. At Cap's.

She glanced across her shoulder and saw McCabe using the shower. She walked into the clearing. Before reaching his pickup, she glimpsed a rectangular plastic object about one-inch wide and three inches in length on the ground near where the sedan had been parked. Next to it was a small square of stiff white paper. She leaned down, collected both objects, and examined them.

The plastic rectangle was a flash drive. She turned over the stiff white paper. The dark-haired man stared at her from his photo on the business card. His name was Tony Underwood, president of Underwood Development Properties in Miami, New York, and Las Vegas.

She sensed McCabe at her side, and as he rested his board next to hers at the rear of the pickup, she handed him the business card. "He was studying the fox dunes area before he and the man he was with drove off." She told McCabe she'd seen their sedan at the lodge.

"Luke told me your grandfather withstood constant pressure to sell the lodge and surrounding land for development. He'd make a bundle if he did, but Luke said the old man was determined to keep the land the way it is." Hands on either hip, he gazed across the wilderness along the coast. "I can see why," he said.

She showed him the flash drive. "I'll need to see what's on here to make sure of its ownership, don't you think?"

He raised his dark glasses, his deep blue eyes locking with hers. "Yes, I believe you must, Eden." He lowered the glasses and pulled his watch cap low on his brow.

At the lodge, McCabe parked beside the east porch. "I'll be out of town for about two weeks. Another lesson is in order when I get back."

"Give me a call," she said.

"It isn't easy to reach you."

"Persistence is a wonderful virtue, McCabe." She thought she saw a slight upward movement at the corners of his mouth, but it was far more likely to have been a trick of the sun's glare. Eden hopped from the pickup and shut its door.

She went looking for Ruth. She wasn't around but her laptop was on the kitchen table, it had been switched on, so Eden plugged the flash drive into one of its ports. The flash drive icon showed up on the desktop. Eden clicked on it and began to review the list of folders displayed. She accessed one and opened the last saved file.

"Oh my God," Eden whispered as she read the file: it was for a multi-million-dollar proposal to buy the lodge and 440 acres of surrounding wilderness along the seashore. There were pictures of the lodge in another folder.

Florida's noteworthy features include sinkholes. They have sucked highways and vehicles into their maws and houses with innocent people sleeping in their beds. Reading the proposal, Eden felt as if she was being sucked alive into one of those terrible sinkholes.

The shock was followed by another when she came across a set of development plans for the property. The plans called for the wilderness to be uprooted and the dunes leveled. Grotesque details said new trees and shrubs would be planted, and a small train was to ferry residents between shopping and recreation areas. The one thing missing from the nightmare was oversized cartoon characters with plastic heads dancing along landscaped pathways.

The sound of a child's laughter drew her away from the kitchen through the dining area and common room to the east porch. Raynell, a bossy six-year-old who had come to visit Ruth, was running along the driveway.

The small square in the child's hand was a camera. If something crawled out of the ocean, if it flew, or spun webs or roamed the dunes wilderness, she would snap its picture. Raynell stopped running when she reached a treehouse and rope swing in the shadows near the stone posts.

CJ had built the little house midway along the sloping trunk of a giant live oak. Eden watched Raynell climb its ladder to the roof. From there the child jumped onto the wide and sturdy trunk and worked her way up into the tree. Jess and Eden used to climb in the canopy of leaves until they could see the dunes where red foxes lived.

If the land was ripped open, the foxes would die and all the wildlife living in the wilderness along with them. They would be shot, poisoned, slaughtered, their bloodied fur and broken bones crushed into the earth beneath relentless wheels. Birds would fly away from felled trees, the trees with exposed roots like skeletal hands begging to be spared before they were ground to dust. The sea would turn brown from runoff. The beach would become a graveyard for sea turtles, for sharks and dolphins, for ancient horseshoe crabs. Some part of everyone would wither inside the new development, surrounded by carefully sprayed and pruned bushes and walls replacing the untamed wilderness.

Raynell's slender legs dangled from a thick limb. Below, Johnny examined the swing's rope. Bobby Hayes gave a cheerful wave to Johnny and Raynell before continuing across the road. He carried a towel and reading material as he headed to the beach. Adam and Adele Winston soon caught up with him.

It was a peaceful clear day of sunlight on the green ocean, a day when men with pleasant faces in bland conference rooms went about making plans to wreck the earth, to tear apart its beauty to fatten greasy wallets and gorge their comfortable bellies. Raynell's children could glimpse the wilderness from their mother's photographs. There would be nothing else left. Eden's nails bit into her palms.

She walked from the porch to the kitchen. She closed the computer, taking the flash drive with her, and she walked up the stairs to Jess's room. Her shoulders were bowed with the awfulness of what she had learned. Jess, CJ, and Luke would never permit a sale or development. Aunt Billie would, though. She had never cared for the lodge.

She felt herself drifting and alone. The lodge probably for sale, Aunt Billie's ownership claim: it was too big to deal with. Eden reached for her backpack and rummaged around for the capsule container. Some small movement, slight as the shadow of a bird flying by the window, made her look up and across the room.

The fox stared at her from its poster on the wall. She saw in its expression the need to be true to herself. She returned the backpack to the closet. After moving the storage cabinet, she lifted the covering from the compartment concealed in the closet floor.

There was plenty of room for her new finds even with CJ's papers and the liner pages covering the unfinished bottom of the compartment. She slipped the developer's flash drive inside and went downstairs. Before long she was on the wilderness path, heading to the southwest. She wanted to stay as far away from him as she could. But there was no way she could avoid it: she had to confront him.

Chapter Sixteen

She had stumbled on a root while hurrying to reach him before he could climb in the Chevy and take off. Trying to ease the pressure on her throbbing ankle, Eden leaned against the porch railing outside his cabin. He glanced at her across his shoulder.

"I've got to be somewhere, Eden," he said, his gaze traveling to her lips and breasts. He would spare her at most a minute out of his important day. "What's it about?"

"The lodge, sir." This got his attention.

He turned around fully, his eyes glinting. "Let us get something straight. The lodge is your aunt's concern. I offer her direction from time to time when she asks for my ideas on how to manage, and she usually ignores whatever I say," he said, the helpless lift of his shoulders at odds with the fixed look in his eye. He had always presented himself as the great fighter and hunter, and he was taking direction from her alcoholic aunt? Eden did not believe him.

"I'm already late," he said. He had to work at opening the car door. The Chevy's doors could be counted on to stick. It gave her more of a chance to talk with him.

"Excuse me, Cap, but I'm sure you are aware of the Miami developer in town wanting to buy the lodge and property. I'm wondering, is there a deal already for its sale?" The slow rattle of cicadas fell away through the trees to a listening silence.

He ducked inside the car, draping an arm over the steering wheel, a booted foot planted in the sandy dirt. He stared through the windshield into the trees. Eden did not get the feeling he was admiring them. His flushed face had taken on a deeper shade of plum.

He tilted his head toward her. A slow smile crept across his face. "Eden, you're a real cute gal. You and I are going to share a meal one day, and I believe you'll like it fine." Eden wanted to laugh.

"About the lodge. Developers come to town all the time looking for bargains, and this place, rundown like it is, qualifies as such. From all she has gone through, especially Jess's disappearing act and Luke and CJ's deaths, your aunt's health is delicate, leaving me with the unpaid burden of managing our opportunities and options. It's a big thankless job."

Eden realized she had caught him in a contradiction. "Well, sir, it could be you were being modest, but earlier you said you offered occasional direction to Aunt Billie about the lodge when she asks. You said she usually ignores you, but from what you told me, it sounds like you're the man in charge."

He brushed at the sleeve of his camo shirt and smoothed his silver hair. "Doesn't matter what I said. She is the boss lady. By the way, have you made any progress with CJ's medals? I guess not or you'd have told me."

"Still looking," she said. She felt certain Cap or someone working for him had spied on her and later taken CJ's papers. But if they had, the papers most likely turned out not to be what he had been searching for.

He narrowed his eyes. "I trust you are enjoying your job and your free room and board? Billie and I hope you won't abuse those privileges by wasting time poking into lodge affairs." He gazed at her mouth.

The message was clear. Eden should be grateful to have a job. Who was she to ask questions about the lodge? She didn't have a legal say in anything to do with it. She understood this. But it had been her home.

He hadn't said it in so many words, but she sensed he meant she ought to stay off any subject having to do with the lodge, including the subject of Jess. Except she also got the clear message he would take a somewhat more lenient view of her inquiries if she went along with certain things he might want from her.

Cold rage rose in her chest. She had not forgotten the time he'd forced himself on her.

He had some nerve while speaking of her family's tragedies to focus on money and the "unpaid burden of managing" he said he was shouldering. Jess had told her he lived rent-free in the cabin because of his relationship with Aunt Billie. It disturbed Eden how he had spoken about Jess, making her disappearance seem like it was a selfish whim on her part. Eden decided she best keep her mouth shut for the time being or she might say something she would regret. Like calling him what he was: a filthy cheating scumbag.

She watched as he swung his leg inside the car and closed its door, turning the key in the ignition. The engine rumbled to life. "Trust your Uncle Cap like you always used to. The lodge is in good hands. Jeez, Eden, you sure have grown up. You have filled out real nice. Listen, anything we've talked about, let us keep as our little secret."

He changed the subject. "Would you do some housekeeping at my cabin? Some dusting, and the dishes? I'll pay extra." People's moods could shift like the weather.

The Chevy disappeared along the winding drive, Cap tossing her way a series of casual loosefingered waves while directing the car toward the stone posts and the road. Eden was thinking it was unlikely he would have invited her into his place if there was anything of interest for her to find. It was best not to expect big results from snooping around. Even so, a possible lack of results was no reason to hold off making a search for drugs and documents.

Eden hobbled up the porch steps while thinking about Cap avoiding her question about a sale of the lodge, thinking also about needing to sit down to relieve the pressure on her ankle. She hoped he still had chairs.

All he had said was she should trust him when he said the lodge was in good hands. She doubted this. He had asked her not to talk with Aunt Billie about the lodge, mentioning her health as the reason. She thought this over. Eden decided she would never use the word "delicate" to describe anything about her aunt including her health. On the other hand, all these years Aunt Billie could have been hiding a deep sensitivity, the party girl masking her true inner self. It was possible. Everyone wore masks.

Eden opened the door and went inside. There was no furniture in the big room except for the dining room table and two chairs. A few picnic coolers and packing boxes were over by the walls.

She opened them and looked inside. They were empty.

She traced a stomach-turning odor to the kitchen and a plastic bag, the bag revealing fish remains inside. Eden removed the fish. She retied the bag and left it in a cart at the side of the cabin. Then she scattered the remains of the fish. The foxes and raccoons were going to have a feast.

Eden washed and dried the dirty dishes and put them away. Other than the overripe garbage and dirty dishes, the kitchen didn't produce anything suspicious: no granules in sandwich bags, needles, weight scales, papers, pipes, or other drug paraphernalia. She had gone through all the drawers, cabinets, and cupboards. Then she surveyed his bedroom. The furniture was gone. The closet and bathroom had been cleaned out.

Her ankle throbbed, and she pulled up a chair to the dinner table and sat with her leg propped on the other chair. She grabbed the remote and clicked on the TV. From an open window the sound of cicadas floated to her before the drone of newscasters' voices took over. It was as if the cicadas did not want her to forget them in the noise and clamor of desperate human activity projected on the screen.

Orange flames poured from a car crash west of Magnolia Beach. There had been a shooting involving drugs at a park and another gun incident stemming from a domestic dispute, both farther south. A persistent brush fire to the northwest on the other side of a bridge separating Magnolia Beach from the rest of the county was in the news. The scent of it had been in the air for days. Eden thought how police and firefighters everywhere were overworked, and how the people they served were often deeply troubled. She wondered how everybody got through all their days.

Following a commercial break, the newscast resumed with pictures of smiling officials from a coastal town wielding shovels at a groundbreaking ceremony. A hotel was to be constructed where another had been destroyed by fire along with a popular boardwalk.

In its heyday the boardwalk drew crowds with its dance hall, arcade, bars, and rides. But changing times, storms and fire ended the seaside amusement park's existence in 1988 along with the old Golden Cove Hotel.

Eden leaned forward, a memory coming to her of golden wavelets and the initials GC Hotel printed on a matchbook cover. She had found it on the floor while cleaning Bobby Hayes's room. She wondered if he had been to the old hotel. It may have been left by another guest.

The sore ankle kept her seated. From beneath the brochures and magazines on the table, the edge of a photograph caught her eye. She pulled it out and studied the picture. It was of a younger Cap in a Navy uniform. His chest was loaded with enough medals to make a fully decorated Christmas tree look bare.

The picture was inscribed to Eden's aunt. Over the years Eden and Jess saw him at happy hour and dinner devotedly sitting with Aunt Billie. He always made sure her glass was full. The thinking was they would marry.

But the years had gone by and there had been no ring on her finger, no walk down the aisle. Her aunt had said there had been many girls in Cap's life. Eden figured he'd gotten the picture out to show off to another woman.

She set the photo next to his antique typewriter. There was paper in it. Eden typed a few lines, remembering how the machine's keys produced uneven lines of type, and how Jess ignored this and went about composing stories for Eden. Jess told her once she wanted to be a writer. "I'll use an old typewriter like this one or a pen on paper," she'd said, "the way writers used to do it."

A wave of sadness came over her in the half-light as she thought of Jess sitting at the table, shaping a story for her. The rising song of cicadas brought her back into the room. She stood up, seeing in the dimness the animals Cap had shot and mounted on the wall. No amount of cleaning and dusting would ever make this cruel place clean.

She went into his study off the kitchen. This room had not yet been cleaned out. Eden glanced at the maps of battles and busts of stone-faced military men. She studied the medals displayed on velvet and hanging like pictures on the walls. Some of them might have belonged to her grandfather. But there was no identification.

There had been hot and dusty Florida afternoons when the cousins and Johnny, looking for something to do, would find their way to Cap's door. He would lead them around and show them his guns and knives. She looked at them as they gleamed from racks and inside glass-top cases.

She found his Walther P38 pistol dating from World War II. It had topped his list of prized weapons. "I killed a Nazi and took the weapon from his bloody hand," he had told them when they were little kids. Eden guessed he was probably somewhere in his sixties, and for the first time she realized he would have been born after the war. There could be a misunderstanding or an explanation for his claim. She could not think of one.

She opened his desk drawers not expecting to find much but filled with unreasoning hope her search would turn up something she could identify as a will.

The drawers were empty. She found on his desk some drinking glasses, the rims smeared with lipstick. She took them with her and headed to the kitchen to give them a wash.

The day was hot and moist, settling with a smothering grayness. She hobbled to Cap's refrigerator in search of bottled water. Six-packs of expensive imported beer jammed its shelves. Tap water would do.

She opened the freezer to grab some ice and found herself looking into the staring eyes of clear-wrapped frozen fish. There were dozens of them, neatly stacked like boards. Eden was not convinced the presence of so many dead fish in his freezer indicated he'd become seriously health-minded. The way his stomach bulged over his pants belt suggested otherwise.

A sudden scraping sound and the clatter of objects falling to the floor sent her to the door. Raynell was near the kitchen on her knees reaching under a table.

"Are you okay? What happened?"

"Nothing got broke." She stood up, dusting herself off. "Miss Eden," she said, her eyes bright with determination, "you've been here a long time. You should come with me."

Eden sensed in her what she once felt when she wanted Jess's company: come swim with me. Let's go to the treehouse. Tell me a story. Show me how to fix my hair so it will look exactly like yours. You are my heart.

Eden meekly followed the dictatorial youngster to the front of the cabin. "Where to?"

Raynell pointed in the direction of the lodge. She grasped Eden's hand in a tight grip and pulled her along outside.

"You don't need to call me miss when you say my name."

Raynell gave her a big smile.

In the kitchen, Raynell settled in a chair and opened Ruth's laptop. Soon she was pointing out close-ups of a starfish and pools of water filled with shells. She clicked on a picture showing the slope of the big dune near the boardwalk. There was an odd shadow near the edge of an area of thick undergrowth and weathered trees.

Raynell swung her legs beneath the chair. "The shadow had a cold," she said, frowning.

Eden was puzzled by the fanciful thing Raynell had said. "What do you mean?" she asked as Ruth stepped into the kitchen. She glanced over their shoulders at the pictures on the computer screen.

"Who took those?" she said.

Raynell lifted her head. "I did, ma'am." There was pride in her voice.

"Was someone with you?"

When the child was silent, Ruth gave her a fierce look, her cheekbones putting Eden in mind of blades made of stone. "I thought I told you never to go to the beach alone. Didn't I tell you never to go into the dunes by yourself?"

"From this day on she will go there with an adult, Ruth. We have an agreement."

Ruth ignored Eden. "Raynell, you answer me!"

Raynell lifted her chin. "You didn't say why I shouldn't go."

"A slip of a girl is asking *me* to explain? You need to learn to cook so you will always have work and be able to take care of yourself even if you go on and become a famous photographer, which you will one day. But pictures, no matter how fine, won't put food on the table when you're starting out."

Eden said to Raynell, "She's more worried than angry."

The flecks in Ruth's blue-green eyes blazed. "No, Eden. I am a hundred percent angry and scared because she's in danger there all alone in the dunes."

Raynell slid from the chair and grabbed a long-handled wooden spoon. Standing on tiptoe, she stirred the big pot of soup cooking on the stove. She did not bother to look her way when Eden called goodbye.

Much later, after Eden had served and cleaned up from dinner and Ruth had gone to her room off the kitchen, Eden slid Underwood's flash drive into the laptop and continued exploring his files. It was then she came across a scanned copy of a letter from someone identified as the Fox Dunes Lodge Trustee.

The letter was addressed to Underwood. If Underwood offered a six-figure bonus and made the trustee a partner in the dunes and lodge development project, the trustee vowed to guarantee a quick sale at a bargain price. The irregularities of the scanned typed letter suggested it had been produced by an old machine in need of repair. Eden knew of one meeting this description.

***

Illuminated by the flashlight Cap had once given her, the typewriter's keys moved onto the sheet of paper with a halting stiffness. She typed several more lines to make sure she had what she would need for a comparison with the scanned letter from Underwood's flash drive. When she was done, she considered taking another look around the cabin, but the sound of a car on the drive ended any thoughts of further exploration.

Headlights probed the cabin walls with the vehicle's rapid approach. She folded and shoved the typing sample into her jeans pocket. As an afterthought, she grabbed the picture of Cap in his Navy uniform. The headlights filled the cabin as she made her way to the back door and down the steps.

Her sore ankle slowed her down. Outside, she had flattened herself against the cabin wall when Cap pulled up in the Chevy.

It took him several shoves to get its door to open and shut. He started up the stairs. If he'd had any reason to look to his right, he would spot her. He went inside. Behind him the headlights from another car swept the drive. It was a black sedan, and it slowed and parked nearby. It would have been too chancy for Eden to make any moves.

A wedge of light from the cabin revealed the snub-nosed profile of the man who stepped from the sedan. The last time Eden had seen the man, he was with the developer Underwood on the walkway at the dunes.

Eden crouched below an open window. From the low murmur of the two men's voices, she heard a few words including "acreage," and "lake." She was aware of the sounds of the forest, of crickets, cicadas and frogs, the whine of mosquitoes. The low mumbling of voices and the clink of ice in glasses floated to her from the cabin.

She heard the flaring of a match striking a wooden box. Soon the pungent odor of weed floated to her. She wondered if Cap had supplied it and if so where he kept it. She was annoyed with herself not to have done a more thorough job of searching the cabin, but it could be he had brought it with him from wherever he lived. Or the other man might be sharing.

It wasn't long before Cap's voice became loud enough for her to hear him calling the other man "Dude," switching to "Mitch" as an argument about the need for cash started to heat up.

She waited to see if Mitch would display some of the temper he had demonstrated at the boardwalk when he was with Underwood. Or if Cap would become angry the way he had with Scooter at the pier. Instead, a long silence settled into the room, as if the night anticipated trouble. The silence was broken when Mitch insisted on more documents.

"It isn't enough," he said. If a mosquito could talk, it would sound like Mitch. His voice was high-pitched. It poked at the darkness like a needle.

She was getting ready to melt into the forest, thinking the two men were still in the main room getting high, when a light went on at the back of the cabin in Cap's study. She watched him take a handgun from a case and inspect it.

She heard a toilet flush. Then Mitch entered the room, and Cap handed the weapon to him. He took another for himself. Armed with flashlights and guns, the two men left the cabin by the kitchen door and walked unsteadily in the direction of the lake.

Sweat soaked her shirt. The penetrating odor of decaying vegetation filled her nostrils. She followed a familiar trail close to the lake. The trail allowed her to keep track of the men and their lights without the need to use the flashlight she carried.

In the darkness, saw-like palmetto leaves cut into her flesh. Mosquitoes bit her ankles and neck. She was afraid of making a sound, so she trod carefully on the dried leaves and boughs underfoot. Loud splashes from the lake announced an alligator going after a doomed creature. All around Eden the wilderness pulsed with hunger, with life. And death.

Eden heard shots fired. The echo faded and she heard laughter. More shots followed. Through the bushes she saw Cap and Mitch directing the beams of their flashlights at something on the ground. It was long and pale and still.

They nudged the 'gator's body with their shoes, laughing as if death was a joke. They stood a moment, Cap pointing across the lake at the forest growing beyond a mound of an island, Cap saying something to Mitch, Eden wishing she knew what it was.

Then they weaved through the forest toward the cabin. Live oak leaves and fallen palm boughs crunched beneath their heavy footsteps. With a bitter taste in her mouth and her heart rocketing in her chest, Eden made her way toward the lodge.

A stamped envelope addressed to her waited on the kitchen table. It was another anonymous message. "My desire for you is growing. Do not make the grave mistake of disappointing me when I make myself known."

Each communication was more threatening than the last. She glanced at the postmark. It had been mailed from a town up the coast where brush fires persisted. She took the letter with her and walked to her room. She turned on all the lights. Then she stood by the window in full view of anyone who might be out there looking in, and she tore up the note.

Chapter Seventeen

Ruth moved her phone aside and whispered to Eden the name "Cyril." She spoke into the phone again, telling Cyril she would call later, and she slipped the phone into the pocket of her jeans. Cyril and Johnny had both come to live at the lodge around the same time. Ruth had raised them as her own. Her body was skinny, her heart as big as the wilderness. She offered shelter for children and animals in need of food and healing.

"What's Cyril doing these days?"

"Teaching. They keep him busy at MIT."

"What's his subject?"

Ruth gazed toward a patch of sky visible beyond the window. "He specializes in planets and stars. Eden, he's written books about what is up there and how it came to be. I am looking at one of its mysteries. She's made of stardust," Ruth said.

Eden glanced outside in time to see Raynell hanging upside down from the limb of a giant live oak near CJ's cabin. Raynell snapped a few pictures before righting herself and doing her circus-girl tightrope-balancing act as she walked along the tree limb.

"When you talk to Cyril next, please tell him Eden says hello. He might remember helping me with my studies." Eden settled into a chair at the table where she had been the young man's student. Sometimes Jess would sit with them.

"He'll remember," Ruth said.

She moved to the stove where she stirred the contents of a stew pot. CJ had bought the property and built the lodge while she'd been raising her children in a shack on the land. This was her home. If anyone had a right to learn Underwood's plans for it, it was Ruth.

"There's a developer named Underwood who's trying to buy the lodge and dunes wilderness."

With the spoon raised above the pot, Ruth gazed across her shoulder at Eden. "What does he want to do here?"

Eden could barely suppress her contempt as she described the plans. Ruth listened in silence, commenting after Eden mentioned the small train to transport residents around the development.

Ruth shook her head in disbelief. "I've often thought we need a train in the forest."

"They're going to destroy the wilderness."

She was betting Ruth would be revolted.

"People do need work," Ruth said. Eden sat in stunned silence, unable to believe what she had heard.

Ruth's eyes blazed. "But CJ would never allow such a thing to happen and neither would Jess or Luke," she said. "It's home to so many living things. After Jess saved a fox, CJ told us, 'They are survivors.' He said he'd heard they'd been brought to these parts in the olden days so hunters could shoot them for sport. Whether or not this is true, there aren't as many foxes here as there used to be.

"This might be one of the last homes around here for all sorts of wild creatures. And for what? Because if you ask me, there's nothing to be valued in a condominium. But is a beautiful old tree full of eagles and owls priceless? What about a forest where foxes raise their families?" Her silence answered the questions.

It was the longest string of words Eden had ever heard Ruth put together. "What else have you learned about the so-called development?"

Eden told her about the trustee letter's promise of a quick sale in exchange for a partnership and a hefty sum paid into a bank account.

"Someone's looking out for their own interests. No names, I suppose."

"No, ma'am."

"Hmmm."

Ruth chopped an onion in thoughtful silence before directing Eden to the refrigerator to retrieve a bunch of carrots. Eden fetched the vegetables, handing them to Ruth.

"How did you come to learn the plans for the lodge?"

"I found a flash drive containing information about it at the dunes walkway."

Her eyes latched onto Eden's. "You kids used to go there to smoke and drink and carry on. You are lucky nobody got arrested."

Cyril was cool when others were acting wild. Once when Jess wasn't feeling well, Cyril walked Jess and Eden to the lodge. Eden secretly longed to have Johnny hold her hand the way Cyril tenderly held Jess's as he helped her reach home. But Jess and Cyril couldn't possibly be anything more than friends. Jess had never said otherwise. Eden thought a girl would have to be crazy to want anyone other than Johnny.

"And Raynell's started acting like she's all grown up and thinking she's going over there whenever she wants."

Eden kept her head down. She said nothing to this.

"She is stubborn and disobedient, like two girls who grew up around here." Ruth didn't need to give her any names.

"You were saying you found a flash drive. I have one of those. Go on."

"To see who owned the drive, I looked over some files, and I studied the pictures. It was an incredible find. I still can hardly believe it.

"Then I read the letter from the trustee. I couldn't quote you from the law books as to what trustees do, but it seems to me a title like trustee means someone who's trusted to manage important things. They're not supposed to cut deals strictly for themselves.

"Cap's told me he takes directions from Aunt Billie, but in the next breath he said he had taken on an 'unpaid burden of management' with the lodge. I feel sure he's the trustee working this deal. Cap has control of whatever funds he can get his hands on. Aunt Billie had to beg him to put money in her bank account."

Ruth's light-flecked eyes gleamed. She said, "Billie and Cap worked on CJ to turn over his property and funds to them. I do not believe this happened. He had his secretive ways."

She rubbed some almond-scented lotion on the backs of her hands. "But Eden, if you believe someone's a cheat, you need more than a suspicion."

"Yes, ma'am. I think I have what I need. There was this odd lettering in a typewriter sample I took

153

from Cap's machine. It matched the trustee letter from the flash drive file."

Ruth hesitated before saying, "Anyone at the lodge could've gone over to Cap's and used his dusty old typewriter to draft a letter. I could have been the one to do it." She stared at Eden a long moment before pointing at the laptop on the kitchen table.

"I bought it for both Raynell and myself. And I guess you might as well leave copies on it of those files from Mr. Underwood's flash drive."

***

Eden wished she could tell her it could happen to anyone, but she didn't think this was true. Bad things happened to Kitty the way trash flowed to some parts of a beautiful beach, but not others. The consignment store where Kitty recently got a job after a long spell of unemployment had been robbed.

"Are you okay?"

"Shook up. I'd stepped out for less than five minutes to get coffee."

"They were professionals able to break in and rob the place in a short time. I'm glad you weren't there."

"The door was unlocked." Kitty sounded calm, but she'd had lots of practice shrugging off disasters. After her ex-husband shot her, she had bounced back to everybody's amazement. She had been through firings before, which is what Eden figured would probably happen next.

"I also called about something else. I spotted a man parked in front of your place. He saw me and took off."

"Did you catch the numbers on his plate?"

"No, but there was what looked like orange blobs pictured on it. I'll keep my eyes open for anything more." It had to be a visitor from Florida with pictures of oranges on his license plate.

Eden sometimes woke up worried she was buried under the junk Annie collected, the plastic knives and forks, the paper coffee cups and plates they ate off, washed, and used again, the broken pots and pans, gardening tools, bicycle tires, and used clothing, faulty lamps, along with all the other yard sale items and stuff Annie had found in trash bins.

If the person in the car from Florida returned and broke into their trailer at the Blue Moon, it wouldn't take long before they'd run screaming out the door after seeing the mounds of Annie's precious junk. There was nothing in the trailer anyone, except Annie, would want. The stuff had kept her mother anchored after all the years of wandering. It would give an intruder a heart attack.

"Has anything come in about the trailer's lease?"

"I haven't seen a renewal notice yet. But there's a strip mall with a tanning parlor opening nearby."

"Life doesn't get much better," Eden said.

Chapter Eighteen

Eden and Raynell were walking along the beach when they saw Bobby Hayes. He sat on the sand reading in the shade of a colorful umbrella. Eden called to him. He looked up and waved.

Raynell skipped at her side. "Bobby's nicer than Cap."

"Did Cap do something to upset you?"

Raynell frowned. "There was the sweetest little armadillo next to his cabin. I went over there and was going to take its picture. Cap shouted at me and the armadillo ran away. I asked if I could take a picture of him and the other man he was coming down the steps with."

"Any idea who it was?"

"He had on a cowboy hat. Cap said if I took any pictures, he'd feed my camera to the alligators. The other man laughed, and he told me to go to the lodge and mind my own business or he'd throw me to the sharks."

"Well, some people are horrible, aren't they?" She hoped extreme suffering would be visited on both men for treating a child so unkindly.

"Did they scare you?"

Raynell shrugged. "Nope." She kicked up some sand. "But he made me miss getting a picture of the little armadillo."

"I believe there are more armadillos in the forest. We will find one and you'll get your pictures. Still, I understand it would've been a special picture, the one those mean guys made you miss."

They continued walking north toward the old pier where Jess had taught her to swim, a flight of pelicans moving parallel to them along the dunes.

"When summer's over, where will you go?" Raynell asked.

"To a town outside Chicago."

"Does it have a beach or an ocean?"

"Lots of fields."

"I'd like to take pictures of fields," she said, "and the people and big machines in them." Raynell clasped her arms across her chest. "I want to take pictures of so many things."

"I predict you will."

"Not the little armadillo, though."

They walked in silence.

"Will you go to school when you get back to the place with all the fields?"

"I haven't figured that out yet."

A Seahawk helicopter flew out over the water, its rotors whirling. Luke had been a chopper pilot;

CJ had flown jets. Eden loved both men, and she was happy for a moment.

Her attention moved to the horizon where a Navy ship plowed the waves. The ship was going to faraway places, something Eden dreamed of doing one day: Asia and Europe, the Middle East, Africa. South America. She and Annie had lived in a bunch of states before they headed north and landed in Illinois. She liked to think the Blue Moon was the home Annie always wanted. Probably the situation was more like she had grown tired of moving all the time and having to give up the junk she liked to collect. She had wanted to travel the world. She'd had time to see a small part of it. But she left Eden her restlessness. This was her heritage. Thoughts of the Blue Moon had her picturing Kitty.

"You asked what I plan to do when I go back to Illinois. Besides work, I'll spend time with my friend Kitty." Raynell asked who she was, and Eden explained how Kitty was a neighbor who had given her and Annie friendship and shared with them the chocolate banana muffins she liked to make. Kitty made them from scratch about every other week. Unfortunately, she would have plenty of time to make muffins. As Eden had feared, Kitty had lost her job at the consignment shop following the robbery.

"Another thing I'll do is take care of my mama's things." Her garage sale treasures. Eden didn't think she'd find any winning lottery tickets while pawing through Annie's possessions. She hoped she would not find a stash of unpaid bills or notification the trailer lease was about to expire.

"I'm going to take pictures every day for the rest of my life," Raynell said, skipping a few steps. "I have some good pictures of the lodge. I think it may be home to ghosts. I love it there."

"Ghosts?"

"Sometimes at night I hear the floor creaking."

"I've heard it, too. It's probably the wind," Eden said. Still, she would tell Ruth to make sure she locked her door when she and Raynell turned in for the night. Eden did this as part of her routine after waking to what she thought was the sound of the bedroom door handle turning. Thinking it might be Johnny, she had investigated, and found no one there.

Eden faced the sea. She grew aware of a restless feeling like a tide moving through her. The feeling carried with it something from the recesses of her mind, the sudden waking from sleep with Jess at her side and CJ's powerful voice rising from downstairs like an angry wave hitting the bedroom walls.

"Billie, I realize it's a challenge, but try to be honest. The lodge could burn to the ground and you wouldn't care so long as you got enough out of it to buy drinks for yourself. You'll sell first chance you have. Unless you have a change of heart, I'm leaving it to someone who values this place." As she walked with Raynell, Eden heard again Aunt Billie's tearful shouts. Jess had slept through it all.

Jess. She was CJ's favorite. Eden gazed toward Red Parker's Reef. She felt her own smallness beside the sea under the sun, and she thought of Jess and tasted the salt of jealousy and sorrow. What she had remembered was evidence of nothing except the troubles between CJ and Aunt Billie.

Raynell raised her camera and snapped Eden's picture.

"You're staying with me. Forever."

Raynell was hopping around, spinning, and jumping, and Eden saw she was a child at the beach, birds circling overhead, and from the water lights hinting at hidden kingdoms under cool emerald-green waves.

Eden thought of telling her there was no "forever." But she could not bring herself to say this. The child's world was already sadder because she was never again going to see a particular armadillo she had fallen in love with.

They waded in the surf, and they walked along the beach, collecting shells, Raynell taking many pictures. In the distance, Bobby Hayes packed his beach gear.

Raynell pointed beyond him along the coast.

"The waves glitter," she said. Eden looked, and thought of golden wavelets on a matchbook cover. When work wasn't keeping her in the kitchen and he was still on the porch talking with other guests, she might ask Bobby Hayes if he knew anything about the hotel with the colorful name.

***

Kitty couldn't talk for long because she was expecting a call from someone she had met. His name was DeWayne, and he was taking her to dinner. "I had to tell you my news," she said. Eden hoped this date would cheer her up after the consignment shop firing.

She ended the call with Kitty before asking if anything had come in the mail regarding the trailer lease. The return call switched to Kitty's voicemail.

Chapter Nineteen

The black sedan with tinted windows sat abandoned in a weedy lot. Eden recognized the car; she walked over for a closer look. Clouds of flies buzzed around it. The smell had her backing away. She heard the wail of a siren. Within seconds, a single cruiser swooped to a stop at the curb. From the shadow of a dumpster she watched a policeman climb from the cruiser, walk to the sedan, and pop its trunk lid.

She saw the crumpled bloody thing inside. A crowd gathered. Eden stepped away, and she walked to a nearby restaurant where she sat at a table waiting for Johnny. They were to meet, and he was going to buy her lunch.

But after a second glass of water, she decided not to wait for him any longer. Everywhere she looked people were talking with their mouths full of raw red meat. She had to get out of there.

Walking north through town to the lodge, Eden decided the dead man did not deserve to be shot multiple times even though he'd planned to destroy the lodge and surrounding land for his development. He didn't deserve to have his body left to decompose in the trunk of the sedan with its purple-tinted windows.

She spoke to Underwood silently as she walked to the lodge. Fate had been too good for him. She told Underwood in her opinion he should have plunged to hell alive and kicking in a sinkhole, screaming until mud filled his lungs and stopped up his mouth.

Not far from the restaurant, she reached a dirt driveway serving the pastel-colored row of apartments where Johnny lived. A white utility van pulled out and stopped at the end of the drive, blocking her way.

The window whirred open, the driver staring at her while talking on the phone. He lifted his mirrored glasses and gave her a familiar smile, managing to be apologetic, boyish, and charming all at the same time. His eyes were the glinting green of worn sea glass.

"Hey, thanks for the information," Johnny said as he ended the call. "Eddie, there's been a murder." He studied her.

"I saw the body."

Johnny leapt out and flung his arm around her shoulder, steering her onto the passenger seat.

"You look like a ghost."

"What else is new?"

"I don't guess you're still interested in lunch."

"The corpse was all shot up. It reminded me of raw hamburger meat. So of course what I want is lunch at a burger place."

"I'll take you to the lodge."

He uncapped a bottle of cold water and handed it to her. The radio was blasting rock. Eden gave him a tight glance, and he switched it off. Music, sunlight, laughter, all of it felt awful. Even the pink bougainvillea they were passing by made her eyes hurt with its neon brightness.

It would be better if she could find a cave to lie down in for a long time. The social worker she knew would ask if she felt she might harm herself, and she would have told him no, she was tired. It could be she lacked a healthy attitude, but she did not care. She would snap out of it. She always had.

Every so often he glanced across the seat. "I didn't mean to stand you up, Eddie. I don't have any excuse except time got away from me. I should've been there to protect you."

"Listen, Johnny, if you have information about my needing protection from an old dead guy stuffed in a car trunk, please tell me. I'm guessing, but I might be able to turn it into a moneymaking situation."

"You're cold sometimes, Eddie. I was trying to apologize, and you won't let me. You turned what I said into a joke."

The boughs of palms lining the street were turning brown in the extreme heat. Everything looked dead. She checked the sidewalks for dead birds, feeling quite sure their stiff feathers and little pink feet had been swept into a drainage ditch.

His voice cut into her thoughts. "The guy wanted to buy the lodge and dunes."

"How'd you learn so quickly?"

Johnny cut a glance at her. He said, "I guess you think I'm the one who killed the guy based on my finding out who he is so soon? Like I'm a hit man? Hey, the money's good. But you forget, word travels fast around a small town."

Eden wasn't at all sure what to believe. Johnny might have a confidential source in the police department, and both Johnny and Underwood knew Cap. Cap might have become fed up and plugged him because the developer wasn't playing ball to his liking. Whatever the case, Johnny was defensive.

Her phone indicated she had a text message from Ted: "U need 2 let go of Us. But I am always here for you. Cheers!" He was "here" for her? What a laugh. Even if she had told him about the corpse in the car trunk, Ted would have sent the same message, complete with exclamation mark. She finally understood he did not love her and never had.

She slipped the phone into her pocket.

Johnny must have read the bleak expression on her face. "The husband back in Illinois?"

"Last time I checked I hadn't stashed any in the other forty-nine states."

By the time he guided the van past the entry posts to the lodge, she was thinking over her decision to head south to Florida after Annie's death. From a financial point of view, she'd thought taking the lodge job was a good idea since it involved free room and board plus pay and tips.

The room and board part had worked out, but so far there had been no paycheck. And not enough guests for tips to matter, although before they had left, Adele and Adam Winston had written her a check. And Mr. Hayes had given her a tip after she had admired his bright tropical print shirt at dinner. Later, she had talked with him out on the porch about winters in Kansas and Illinois.

"It can get awfully cold on the prairie. I come here summers to recover," Mr. Hayes had said with a shy smile. Winters in Illinois were probably as hard as in Kansas, Eden said, and he agreed. "I've been both places in January," he said. After she left she realized she had forgotten to ask about the Golden Cove.

Her phone buzzed, and she answered. "I'll be in town soon. I'm taking you out to eat at a place I think you'll like," McCabe was saying. Eden had ignored his messages. But she found herself unexpectedly wanting to tell him what had been going on. She wanted his ideas. It was true he was bossy, but they had chocolate donuts in common, and she knew he would show up at the exact day, time, and place he said he would.

She accepted McCabe's invitation.

Chapter Twenty

Johnny coasted to a stop between the shed and the lodge's south porch.

"Who called?"

"A friend of Luke's. From the Navy."

"What's the name?"

"McCabe Jones."

Johnny frowned. "Luke called me one time. He was upset, and he told me he was having trouble with a guy. I couldn't talk long and didn't get a lot of detail because the connection was off. Anyway, the name's familiar."

"They served together overseas."

"Luke said he and the guy fought about something to do with Jess, but like I said, the connection was bad."

"Did Jess ever mention the name?"

Johnny shrugged. "It doesn't mean she hadn't met him from somewhere."

Johnny had stood her up for lunch. The call wasn't any of his business. He was attempting to interfere with a friendship. And she needed friends. Eden was startled to realize she thought of

McCabe as one. It felt like he was trying to help her but not so he could get her in bed. She was probably fooling herself in this regard.

She was halfway across the seat of the van about to jump down when Johnny reached for her arm and held on. "Eddie, don't go," he said.

Eden decided to give him a chance to make things right between them. She relaxed and let him settle his arm around her shoulders. She allowed him to turn her face toward his.

Some part of her resisted, though, and she kept her eyes averted until he brushed a strand of hair from her cheek. His touch was gentle.

"We should be together more, Eddie," he said. He had accepted her when she was scrawny and unlovely. He had told her she was beautiful even though she'd been sobbing and hiccupping seawater and trembling with fear.

Beyond the van window, vines and bushes, bright tropical plants and twisted trees crept closer around the lodge every day, threatening to engulf it. But it was the tangle of her emotions she felt overwhelming her. She was lost in the shadows of her own wilderness.

"Look, it's true I let you down today. Can you find it in your heart to forgive me?"

"Ask me again this time next year. Or better yet, make it the year after."

Johnny frowned. "Luke forgave me for stuff I did." Johnny had punched Luke and Luke had punched him back. A couple of times. She had seen both red-faced and doubled over, bleeding, and she knew Johnny hit hard. So did Luke. Later Eden heard Luke telling his friend to forget what had happened between them. It was no big deal. They were like brothers.

He helped her out of the van. Eden imagined she was stepping from a horse-drawn carriage instead of from a utility vehicle. She was a lady instead of a tomboy with raised welts from the mosquito bites she had scratched on her legs and arms. She let him pull her to him. She lifted her gaze to his.

They kissed, their lips warm and seeking. He tried to guide her into the van again, but she drew back, and he leaned against the vehicle door, his thumbs hooked in the belt loops of his jeans. He studied her.

"There's a party at Kathy's this weekend. Will you let me give you a ride?"

"If I walk, I might get there."

"You're awful tough on me." His smile was sweetly sad and sexy.

"What's her address?"

He gave her the street and number. "It's five miles south of here."

Five miles? She might want to rethink Johnny's offer.

***

Aunt Billie, propped against a stack of pillows on her unmade bed, poured whiskey into a glass and set the bottle next to a pot of orchids on a crowded bedside table. One more cigarette pack, glass, or bottle on the table and the pot would tip over onto the floor, possibly breaking the plant's long stem and destroying its delicate flowers.

Eden thought how small, lovely things had a way of showing up even in the unlikeliest of places, her aunt's bedroom being one of them. Clothes and used food containers were on the floor. The closet stood wide open with the contents spilling out.

In the middle of it all was this pot of orchids, as if the flowers believed they had a duty to thrive and make things beautiful because so much of everything else was an ugly dirty shambles. Eden slid the pot away from the edge to a safer place on the table. She didn't have a lot of hope for the plant's future. She considered stealing it.

"Cap says there's no money to pay you," Aunt Billie said. She studied the rim of her glass before tossing the drink down and pouring herself another. "I sure hope there'll be more long-staying guests soon," she said, turning the glass in her hand. "We'll have money then." She avoided Eden's gaze.

Eden knew Ruth would have told her if there had been calls for reservations. She asked anyway. "Any prospects?"

"If so, nobody's mentioned it." She gave the room's middle distance a long, bleary stare. "The thing of it is, Jess always wanted more even though we gave her what we could. This is a lot of the reason why we're in the trouble we're in. You're family, too. Don't you go and be like Jess."

Eden nearly walked out. The hypocrisy of her aunt suggesting Jess drove her to the poorhouse was outrageous. Jess was mostly unpaid. And it was ridiculous the way her aunt was playing the member-of-the-family card. Summers when Eden visited, Aunt Billie had barely noticed her except to send her to the kitchen for more pizza and beer for guests.

Her face was deeply lined and puffy. It was clear the Bahama Blasters and coffee brandies along with the Florida sun were catching up with her aunt. Eden thought about the police report describing Jess's plea to be allowed more time with friends. And she wanted to be paid. Some of the lodge money should have gone to Jess, but it had gone down Aunt Billie's throat.

"Was there someone you think might have wanted to hurt her, Aunt Billie?" It was always possible her aunt would have more to say about her daughter's disappearance than the last time Eden had the opportunity to raise the subject.

"She could sometimes be moody like her—like your mother, so anything's possible." She inspected her fingernails. "I can't name anyone, though. About everyone liked her, at least they said they did."

Clearly, not everyone liked Jess. For instance, Aunt Billie and Cap.

Her aunt got up off the bed and went to a window. Eden followed. The lodge was visible in all its decay, its chimney leaning into the blue sky. Eden was not prepared for what happened next.

Aunt Billie's hand shook as she lifted her glass: "Here's to the lodge. I busted a gut for it, I earned the right to it, and it's all mine. Don't you forget it." She kept her watery gaze on Eden and drained the liquid before doubling over, wheezing.

Eden understood her aunt was referring to her years as entertainment chief, but the toast was so confrontational she thought there had to be more to it. When Cap had warned her not to talk with Aunt Billie about the status of the lodge, she had decided she would have to speak with her at length on the subject, and this was the perfect time. Aunt Billie had brought up the subject.

"Aunt Billie, are you going to make any changes to the lodge?"

"I might paint a few rooms," she said. Her shrug was indifferent.

"Are you thinking of selling?"

"If I get any offers, and I sure haven't, I might consider it," she said. She walked with a halting step to her bed and fell back against the pillows. She jabbed a finger toward the bathroom and ordered Eden to fetch the whiskey stashed there. Eden returned with it to find Aunt Billie's eyes closed and her mouth slack. She took the bottle into the kitchen, setting it in a cabinet. Aunt Billie would have to search for her next drink.

Eden left through the garage and crossed the road. Aunt Billie had spoken with more emotion about her ownership of the lodge than about her missing daughter. But no one had ever been sent to prison on a charge of hardness of heart.

***

When Kitty was excited, she bubbled with information. "I discovered someone messed with the lock at your place and jimmied a screen. I was able to fix everything. Whoever did this was not a professional from Chicago. They didn't get inside." Kitty was scornful.

"Tell me everything," Eden said.

"Things are under control. You remember Melvin, third place down? His dogs' barking alerted the entire neighborhood to the trouble.

He's happy to have a dog stay overnight at your place. One is going to have puppies. It will be a reliable alarm system installed for the price of dog food.

"Oh, and I found some unopened mail addressed to Annie next to the half-dead cactus she kept trying to revive. I didn't see anything with an address from the trailer rental company and nothing's been delivered recently either. I got my job back."

Eden was tempted to mention her idea of a short trip to the Blue Moon, even though doing so on low funds would be somewhat of a challenge. She needed to conserve her pennies since no check would be forthcoming anytime soon, if ever.

Meanwhile, Kitty sounded happy; Eden decided not to burden her with trying to help her figure out how to get the finances for a trip home. Kitty would offer Eden money she did not have. And she certainly didn't want Kitty out walking the streets like she had at one time in her life to pay her bills. This was before she found the preacher who eventually shot her.

"Congratulations, Kitty, on getting rehired at the consignment shop. They shouldn't have let you go in the first place."

"Oh, I do so love talking to you. Listen, honey, I have some other good news." When she filed the report at the police station about the robbery, she had met an old boyfriend from high school.

"Was he behind a desk or behind bars?"

"He's taking me dancing."

"What happened to the other guy you've been dating?"

"DeWayne?"

"Yes."

"He broke a window at my place. I had to ditch him."

"Are you safe?"

"Safe as can be." Her new friend, the policeman, was going to get a restraining order against DeWayne, and the two friends ended the call by telling each other to be careful and stay out of trouble. They both laughed at the thought of anything like trouble being part of lives as tame as theirs.

In Jess's room, Eden pulled aside the cabinet in the corner of the closet and opened the concealed compartment under the flooring. The photo of Cap in his Navy uniform stared up at her.

She set it aside to glance through the papers from CJ's, checking again the scraps of what appeared to be land descriptions, but pages were damaged and missing, making identification impossible. She was ready to replace the papers in their compartment when she glimpsed a folded paper mixed in with the others. She had overlooked it. She gave it a quick read, her heart pounding at what it said. Eden set the letter along with the photo in her backpack and headed out the door.

Chapter Twenty-one

The chip snapped between her fingers, splattering chunks of salsa on the table. Eden was mostly immune to embarrassment having lived with her own awkwardness and with Annie, so she could not explain the heat rising in her cheeks. McCabe glanced toward the kitchen, raising his hand in a commanding gesture of summons, and a waiter hurried to clean the spill before Eden had a chance to do it herself. She gazed past McCabe's shoulder to regain her shaky sense of composure.

A guy sitting nearby nodded in the way men will acknowledge an attractive female, without in any way committing themselves. Eden smiled. McCabe looked to see what she was smiling at.

"Is he an acquaintance?" There was an edge in his tone.

"No. And anyway, I've got a husband, McCabe." She hadn't thought it necessary to tell him this earlier. He was her teacher, her mentor. Nothing more.

"You aren't wearing a ring," he said. There was a question in the statement.

"No, I never have." Eden realized this did not explain her situation. She owed him more. "We've been separated for several months." And married for about the same amount of time. It would be too depressing to mention how she suspected Ted started seeing other girls right after they'd returned from the courthouse.

McCabe studied her face, his expression unfathomable.

It was a good time to change the subject. Eden reached into her backpack and pulled out the photograph of Cap in his Navy uniform covered with medals. She handed it to him across the table.

"There's something strange about this picture. I thought you might tell me what you think."

McCabe carefully examined the photo. It didn't take him long to return it to her. "It's an example of what happens when a kid goes wild in a candy store. He buys too much of everything and then crams it all in his mouth. The man's wearing medals from every branch of the military from different wars. It's not likely."

The waiter brought a tray of food and set their plates on the table along with more chips and salsa.

"When we were kids, he told us stories about saving his men. He showed us his gun collection and the medals he told us he was awarded. He was our hero."

McCabe handed the photo to her. "Wearing unearned medals and making up stories about an unimpressive or nonexistent service record is lying. Kids are easy targets. Adults are taken in many times, too. I bet he wanted to impress a woman with this nonsense. If money is involved, it could mean time behind bars."

Eden reached into the backpack and removed the document she'd discovered folded over and tucked in with the other papers in the closet compartment. McCabe read the letter. When he had finished reading, he handed it back. "It's addressed to CJ. Isn't he your grandfather?"

"Yes. I'm thinking CJ caught Cap in a lie and decided to write the National Archives and Records Administration requesting service record information. Or Jess wrote the letter under CJ's name."

The archives letter stated there were no records for a George "Cap" Williams having been in any branch of the service.

"It's possible his files might have been lost or destroyed. But I'd say the photo together with the letter suggest he never served one hour in the armed forces."

"He raises money for veterans. You'd think someone would've tripped him up about his record."

"He was smart enough to not speak of his fabricated record at public events. He probably never wore the medals or bragged about missions and saving his men. Except to little kids. Their parents might have thought they'd gotten their stories wrong if the kids told them what he'd claimed."

"CJ admired his social skills."

McCabe took a sip of coffee and set the cup down. "This guy Cap's a smooth operator. A good portion if not all the money he raises I'm willing to bet makes its way into his personal bank account. He could be a problem if he learns someone's found out he's a fake."

Winters in Illinois, freezing winds blow across the fields. Looking at him, Eden thought McCabe was traveling somewhere with a cold wind. "Lying to children. Taking money from guys probably suffering from PTSD, guys who served." He took a bite of his taco, set it down, chased it with water. "The guy's a con."

"Jess had no regard for Cap. She may have found out about his lack of a service record and confronted him."

"Could be."

Eden decided not to tell McCabe her suspicions about Cap's drug dealing. She had a hunch but no specific evidence. It was a strong one, but there were other things on her mind, like Cap appearing to make the lodge his.

"Remember the flash drive we found? Everything you've said about him seems to fit in with what's on it. And a conversation I overhead," Eden said.

"You're the one who found the flash drive," McCabe said. "Tell me all you've learned."

She described the proposal to buy the lodge property and the scanned letter from the unidentified trustee offering a cheap sale in exchange for a partnership with the development company and a hunk of cash. The letter had been typed on Cap's old machine. She described the talk she'd overheard of documents and money between Mitch and Cap.

"Cap has a lot of travel brochures in his cabin. I believe he's going to sell, pocket the money, and go for an extended vacation to the Caribbean. I suspect Aunt Billie won't be at his side in her bikini."

McCabe said, "Your aunt might have given him permission to negotiate."

"It's possible. But she didn't seem aware of any offers when I talked to her last. Also, my grandfather thought Aunt Billie would sell after his death. And he was vehemently opposed to a sale. He didn't believe in the courts, and a reliable source thinks there's a will hidden at the lodge."

McCabe thought this over. "Cap may be cheating your aunt out of a lodge she's pretending to own."

The waiter came with the bill. McCabe stood up and pulled a credit card from his wallet. A snapshot came out of the wallet along with the credit card. It fell on the table, landing directly in front of Eden.

She glimpsed the picture of a young woman with a baby in her arms. McCabe scooped it up and put it back in his wallet. He didn't say anything about the picture.

They drove to the lodge, Eden thinking about how Luke served his country heroically and paid with his life while Cap was living a life of lies about his service and making money at it. *She didn't care about McCabe's picture of the young woman.* She wanted to believe there had been some good in Cap's relationship with her grandfather, but even his romance with Aunt Billie had likely been no more than preparation for possessing the lodge when CJ grew old and sick. *She didn't care about McCabe.* CJ had died in May. Cap hadn't wasted much time achieving his aim. His likely being a drug dealer was in keeping with everything else he did: he took people's money and turned their lives into hell.

Eden had struggled to tune out McCabe. When he spoke to her she barely heard what he was saying.

"Keep at it, Eden. Don't give up."

"What?"

"Surfing. You'll be riding waves before long."

She sensed his glance in the darkness of the Silverado's cabin, and then his attention was on the turn into the lodge. He'd been useful driving her around and giving her a surf lesson. There'd be more of those if she decided this was what she wanted of him. *She'd be the one to decide.* He'd helped her figure out who Cap really was. All of this was in his favor.

McCabe drove up to the east porch and turned to the right to park alongside the lodge when Eden glimpsed movement reflected in the side-view mirror. A van from the direction of Cap's cabin sped toward the main road. Johnny was at the wheel, his phone clamped to his ear. He didn't bother to look toward the Silverado.

Eden slid across the seat about to open the pickup door when McCabe told her he was leaving on assignment sometime in the next few days.

"I may be away for as long as a week or two. If I decide to get in some flying time, I'll be here much sooner. I'll call when I get back. We'll surf."

"Okay," Eden said. Stepping into the night, she realized she wasn't sure how to navigate anything of importance in her life: discovering what happened to Jess, finding the will, and, if she could, stopping the sale of the lodge. Whatever she felt for McCabe didn't matter. The same could be said for Johnny.

"Take care," McCabe said. Most of the guys she'd gone to school with knew exactly how to deliver the phrase with the right nonchalant tone. McCabe said it with a thoughtful formality. It made her feel the difference in their ages. Eight years at least. Possibly more. It was weird to find herself even thinking about his age in relation to her own.

Eden walked from the Silverado onto the porch steps. From there, she watched the pickup's red taillights vanish at the stone posts. She had started thinking again about the picture of the pretty woman and baby when Kitty's frightened voice came to her in a phone call. "He's stalking me. I'm calling 9-1-1." The connection went dead.

Chapter Twenty-two

It took several calls from Eden, but at last Kitty answered. "The police are here. DeWayne threw stuff around, furniture and food mostly. Anyhow, the place is pretty much unlivable. Broken windows and doors."

"What about you? Did he hurt you?" Eden asked.

"One or two tiny bruises, and you are not to worry."

"Kitty, you go right this minute to the hospital, and then you can stay at my place for however long you need." At least the walls at her rental weren't plastered with food, and Kitty had checked and repaired the windows and doors after the attempted break-in.

"Honey, are you sure?"

"How can you even question such a thing? You already have the key. And you've got dogs for protection."

"The dogs are with Melvin. But my friend at the police station said they'd make sure DeWayne never comes near me again. They're going to charge him with something."

"They should put him away forever. Promise you'll go to the ER to get yourself checked out?"

"Oh, it's nothing to speak of." Kitty was in a hurry to end the call. Eden could hear it in her voice. She said she needed to get a good night's sleep and be ready for work in the morning. After what Kitty had been through, Eden couldn't imagine how this would be possible.

Hearing what had happened to her friend was unsettling; she decided the thing to bring her some calm would be a walk along the beach.

She jumped across gullies left by the tides. She dodged seaweed and driftwood. Turning inland at the old pier, she took the walkway above the low shore dunes and over the shallow valley carpeted with flowers. She couldn't see the colors of the flowers in the dark, but she knew their red and yellow faces were looking at the moon.

She wondered if there might be a fox or two out hunting. You had to keep looking to find one. You might not ever this time around, but the rewards were there in the quest itself. She peered into the darkness. The tall-stemmed sea oats covering the dunes whispered in the wind.

When she reached the big dune, she jumped from the walkway and climbed the sandy slope, settling midway up and facing the sea. A ship glided along the horizon. A helicopter flew above, its navigation lights flashing. Music was coming from the clearing behind her. She retraced her steps to the walkway and went to investigate.

Inside a circle of cars, young people danced.

A figure stood at the edge of the circle looking like a dad hanging out with the kids, a golf shirt tight across his middle. He was bald. Eden didn't recognize him until he'd finished brushing off the cowboy hat he held in his hand and had settled it on his head. She walked over.

"Hey, Scooter."

"Well hey, little lady," he said, his eyes making a slow trip from her mouth to her feet and back again with a rest stop at her breasts. "You're looking good," he said. There was always the chance she might learn more about Jess, and when he asked for a dance, she left her backpack on his pickup's front seat, breathing in the expensive leather smell before joining him.

Scooter was as good a dancer as she remembered. Soon they were surrounded by a clapping audience. When they finally took a break, Eden and Scooter propped themselves against the pickup. There was a big cooler sitting on its bed. He half turned from her to pour a beer into a large paper cup. He handed it to her with a low bow. A young man separated himself from the crowd and walked over.

He wore his jeans riding on his hips, a thin cotton shirt open in the front except for a single button below the middle. His curly hair bounced on his shoulders. Scooter nodded toward a place over by the dune where trees grew thick. The young man walked there. Scooter followed. They were gone long enough for money and product to change hands.

When he returned, he offered Eden a ride to the lodge. They drove under a canopy of twisted live oak heavy with trailing moss. At the side of the dirt road beneath leafy vines and fallen tree limbs, animal eyes glowed in the headlights.

It wasn't clear to her when he had lit up or if she'd taken a long inhale. But she couldn't stop laughing at how cleverly he had managed to drive for hours along the same remote stretch of road. His driving was slow enough for it to feel like he had parked. She was halfway paying attention to him when she heard Scooter's nasal voice.

"You could do it, easy. If you decide to, you'll need a portfolio. I can help you create one."

"What are you talking about?"

"Modeling."

She gazed at him through the fragrant smoke. "Seriously," she said. Her voice sounded like it came from somewhere outside the pickup.

"I got some great shots of Jess. You always wanted to be like her, didn't you?"

"Jess wanted to go to New York City to find a writing job. She never spent a lot of time on her looks."

"She was desperate for money. And escape. Kathy and I, we felt bad for her, and we tried to help her. We want to help you, too, Eden. It seems like you have fallen into the same trap Jess was in: no money and taken advantage of at the lodge. And you both have talent. You'd make a great model."

Eden laughed, her head nodding forward. There was a small bundle of rags to one side of her left foot. The rags were smeared with a dark stain. A knife blade stuck out of the bundle. She hadn't noticed it.

Scooter threw her a glance.

"Yeah, it's a bloody knife," he said.

What he was came to her then, an insecure man trying to prove his virility. Eden laughed. "Are you trying to scare me, Scooter?"

"It's fish blood, Eden. A fish knife, rags, and fish blood. Like they say, it don't mean a thing."

His voice was bouncing to her from somewhere on the pickup's roof. She wasn't at all sure how it had happened, but he'd gone from talking about the great modeling career he could introduce her to, to telling her of a dive trip he and Johnny took with Jess and Kathy. Things were moving fast.

"We anchored next to one of those islands in the Keys and went night diving. Jess drifted away from us."

"You and Johnny let her get separated from you?" Her voice leapt out of her like an animal bursting from a cage. Jess had been abandoned at sea.

"Hey, Eden, you don't have to yell. I was testing to see if you'd had too much to drink, and I think you have, Eden, and I want to help you. For one thing, you need to stop believing you understand all the things you hear or see. It will get you in trouble. And from how you reacted to those bloody rags and what I was saying about Jess, it's clear you jump to conclusions.

"I'm telling you this again, what happened to Jess is, she ran away. She is out there living a new life somewhere. My sister Kathy was one of Jess's closest friends, and she told the police the same thing. And they think it's what happened, too. Johnny won't say anything different, either." He paused, darting a look at her from across the seat. "Your little investigation won't bring you what you want. The police don't like meddling same as dogs don't like fleas."

The mention of dogs and fleas brought tears to her eyes for dogs everywhere. When she realized she felt bad for the fleas, too, she knew she was in serious trouble. She heard a voice sounding strangely familiar replying, "Yes, you're right, Scooter."

The words were slurred. The voice faint. Eden glanced over her shoulder into the back to see who could be talking. Nobody was there. She was forced to conclude the vaporish sound was her own voice. She was in terrible shape.

He said, "Look, why don't we stop at my place? You could use a cup of coffee. And I'd like to show you my studio."

"All right," she said in the same cloudy voice. She was drunk, drugged, and about to go to his studio. Good thinking.

When they reached his apartment building, he helped her out of the pickup. She laughed and stumbled, and he grabbed her arm and marched her into a place of too many corridors with carpets smelling of cheap newness. It made her eyes water. The elevator swayed. They walked into a room where the walls were covered with floor-to-ceiling mirrors.

Eden struggled to focus. But the umbrella lights on stands, a hot-pink satin backdrop, scattered pillows, blankets, plush toys, and mattresses were all moving around in a strange undulating dance. He held out a roll of bills for her to examine. Not even those would stay still. There was a nasty turbulence in her gut.

He said, "Here, take it," and she watched him count out ten bills with Ben Franklin's picture on them. She felt even more rotten the way Ben was looking at her. Sour and disapproving.

She said, "What's it for?"

"I have plenty of it and you need it. Listen, my money wasn't too good for Billie. Or Jess."

"What?"

Scooter had crossed the room and was leaning over a file cabinet in a corner. He looked back at her across his shoulder. "I promised Billie I'd never do this, but she's a close friend and so are you so I can show you. You'll see this could become a real good family business for the three of us."

"What about Jess?"

"The pictures I took of her are in another location. We'll go there some other time."

He walked toward her, withdrawing some photos from a plain clasp envelope. Apparently there was even a thriving market for sex pictures of older women with wrinkled skin, flabby bellies, and used-up breasts. Eden saw enough to tell her Aunt Billie had posed for Scooter.

"You see, if it's acceptable for your aunt, you should feel the same. And the pay is terrific, Eden."

She needed something, but it wasn't cash. Eden sank to the floor on her knees. Scooter stood over her. She looked up the length of his pant legs. His face expanded and shrank above her. The room tilted.

"You good with this?" he asked. "I can change the look of the set for you," he said, glancing around the room.

"Oh sure," she said, her words sounding thick.

"I don't want you doing anything you're uncomfortable with. It took Billie a while to get used to the routines. But then she got the hang of it, I mean you can see it from the pictures. We'll take a couple of shots. Let me show you how I want you to sit. I'm putting the money away, but I'll make sure you get it before the night's over."

"Right," Eden mumbled.

He reached down and pulled her up off the floor, guided her over to some cushions, then fiddled with the buttons on her shirt. She cringed as his hands touched her flesh. Chunky liquid rushed up her throat, filling her mouth with a sweet acid taste. The liquid gushed from behind her clamped teeth.

"What the hell?" Scooter said, jumping back. He tried to shake off the vomit clinging to his arm and hand. His fingers dripped.

One more robust heave and Eden's head cleared as quickly as it had fogged over. She went into the bathroom and washed her face and hands.

She gargled some of Scooter's mouthwash. She used his towel.

"You can take me home," she said when she returned to the studio. They hadn't gone far when light bars flashing on police cars and orange flares on the ground signaled trouble ahead.

A car had gone into a ditch. Its hood was smashed, windows shattered, the doors flung wide. Police were directing traffic around the wreck. Eden had the sensation she was the one who had spun out of control.

They drove past it. Scooter said, "I thought we had a good talk, Eden. I thought I was helping you become part of a family business. It's a first step, but there are big payoffs. Don't you want a better life? Look, so you got sick, it doesn't bother me. I can drive us back, and you can stay at my place."

"Not until you get a cleaning crew in there." She wasn't sure what made her say what she did next. "Like you did after you killed Jess because she didn't want to cooperate."

Scooter slowed the pickup to a stop. He reached down and grasped the bloody bundle with the straight-bladed knife sticking up like it was part of a bouquet. He set it on the seat between them. In the faint light from the dashboard, it looked as if a nylon stocking had been pulled over his head, masking his eyes, nose, and mouth.

"I like you, Eden," he said, his nasal voice a whisper. "But I might change my mind."

"The police will hear me screaming if you try to stop me." Eden pushed open the door and staggered onto the road. Scooter made a sharp U-turn and sped away.

She walked until she reached the stone posts and drive. From behind the twisted branches of trees swaying with tendrils of moss, the lodge leaned into the night. Its faint yellow lights seemed too far for her to reach.

***

The next day, Eden walked from the lodge across the road. She found Aunt Billie on her bed, a bottle of coffee brandy and a half-filled glass on the little table at her side. The orchid plant was in the wastebasket. She wasn't surprised.

She handed Aunt Billie a copy of the dunes trustee letter to Underwood.

"What's this?"

"It's about the sale of the lodge. Were you aware a sale was being negotiated?"

"Huh?" Aunt Billie snatched the letter from Eden's hand and began reading.

Eden said, "There's no mention of anyone to be included in the deal other than the letter writer. It doesn't seem fair. What do you think?"

Aunt Billie's eyes were fixed on the letter as though unable to process what she read. When she finally looked up, she said, "It's private and personal. It's none of your business."

"You remember the old typewriter Cap has at his place? The letter was typed on it. The developer's dead, but he's got a partner. So the proposal may still be on the table."

Aunt Billie closed her eyes and bit down on her lip.

Eden said, "Cap's a cheat. He brings other women here."

Aunt Billie's shoulders sagged. "So what? Other women wanting him shows I have real good taste."

Eden handed her the picture of Cap in uniform. "I found it under some magazines when I was cleaning his cabin. The cabin he lived in rent-free for years at your expense."

Aunt Billie glanced at it and waved it aside. "He's gotten jowly since this picture was taken, but he's real handsome anyway."

"He's wearing too many medals from too many wars for it to be credible. Oh, and there's one other thing." Eden showed her the letter from the National Archives and Records Administration stating there were no records for Captain George "Cap" Williams ever having served in the military.

Aunt Billie said, "He got carried away trying to impress me. He's my hero."

"Cap's lied to you about who he is, he's cheated on you, and it seems like he's trying to swindle you out of your inheritance," Eden said, giving Aunt Billie the benefit of the doubt on whether she was to inherit anything. "He's been setting you up for years."

"And by the way, is Scooter blackmailing you? I saw the pictures. Aunt Billie, you need to get your hair done."

Circles of blusher shrank like pricked balloons on Aunt Billie's cheeks. She balled her hand into a fist and shook it at Eden. "Get out, you little bitch," she hollered. Eden took her time, leaning down and rescuing the battered orchid from the trash before walking from the room.

Midway into the garage, she heard glass shattering. She crossed the road thinking about broken glass and orchids, and the way blackbirds were circling above the lodge in the serene blue sky.

Chapter Twenty-three

The woman at the doorway moved to one side. Eden stepped over the threshold and followed the woman along a brightly lit corridor. The summer uniform showed off the woman's tanned legs. She made the bulletproof vest she wore look fashionable. But the gun she carried could never be mistaken for a fashion accessory.

Eden entered a small room. Its gray walls and worn gray carpeting were the last sights of freedom for some. After being questioned here, they would be jailed. The room was furnished with a table and two plastic chairs.

Eden sat in one of the chairs. Officer Campbell sat in the other. The police officer faced the exit. Eden faced a wall. From her perspective, there was no way out. She decided the room had been set up this way on purpose.

"What can I do for you?"

"Find my cousin Jess Sinclair."

"We've investigated. There's no evidence of foul play and no reason to believe she's taken her life." Officer Campbell pulled a notebook from a pocket and set it on the table. Her stare was neutral.

"I've been checking social media to see if she'd moved on with life somewhere else," Eden said. "Jess wouldn't use a screen identity. And if she had moved on, one way or another she would have gotten in touch with me or someone else."

Even if Jess had decided to cut Eden out of her life, she wouldn't do this to Ruth. Ruth had been like a mother to Jess.

Officer Campbell said, "There's no law requiring an adult, which your cousin was at age nineteen, has to stay in touch with family or friends. Sometimes people don't want to be found."

Eden described her suspicions about a connection between Jess's disappearance and the sale of the lodge. She told her about Cap raising money from veterans while pretending to be one. Eden said, "Jess may have been about to expose him as a fraud." She handed her the official letter documenting he had no service record.

"Anything else?" Officer Campbell's face was expressionless.

"No, ma'am." But she wasn't giving up.

Officer Campbell said she'd call a detective in the downtown sheriff's office and get his name to her once she'd confirmed he thought he could offer any assistance. The expression on the officer's face told her nothing one way or the other, but for Eden, hearing she would make a call was enough to keep her from breaking down. She followed the officer along the airless corridor and walked out the door. She was grateful Officer Campbell had listened.

Several days later while vacuuming the common room, a headline in the local *Magnolia Beach Ledger* caught her eye: "Policewoman Promoted." She turned off the vacuum and sat down to read about Officer Campbell and how she was going out of town for a training program, effective immediately. She would be away for a month.

Eden folded the paper and continued pushing the machine around the room. When she had finished, she put the vacuum away and walked into the kitchen.

It was waiting for her on the kitchen table. "I grow frustrated with wanting to touch you. I will do it. Soon." Eden crumpled the note and tossed it in the trash.

Chapter Twenty-four

Noise and confusion from the party followed Eden as she went with Kathy upstairs into a bedroom. Pictures of circus animals looked down from the walls. Past a shelf of dolls and beside a window, a child slept in a small bed. One of her arms clutched a toy bear. The bear evidently didn't lack for attention. It was missing a lot of fur.

"My daughter," Kathy said.

Kathy had not been exactly friendly at their first meeting, and Eden had never been able to arrange to have coffee with her. It was surprising, then, when Johnny told her Kathy wanted her to come to the party. It was even more surprising when she got there, and Kathy said she had someone for her to meet.

Eden stepped over to the end of the bed. Kathy moved off across the room, and Eden looked out the window to the beach. Waves sounded with the steady beat of a heart. The stars were tiny fists of sparkling light, and for a moment she let herself believe Jess was alive somewhere in the big world, cradling a child.

She heard Kathy come up behind her. Eden turned to her, remembering Scooter saying he and Kathy both wanted to help her. She didn't think Kathy would make the same suggestion Scooter had about modeling. It could be drugs she wanted to talk about, suggesting to Eden she become a street seller, but not here, and besides, Kathy might not be involved with those businesses.

Still, she was prepared for anything from Kathy after her sudden change in attitude toward her. Earlier, when Eden had walked in the door, Kathy had been gushingly friendly with a hug and many "sweethearts."

Kathy's eyes were fixed points shining at her from the darkness. She wanted to get something across the way an archer wants to send arrows into a target.

Kathy leaned over and pushed a lock of hair from her daughter's forehead. Angela smiled in her sleep. There was something strikingly familiar in the smile. "Jess ran away," Kathy said. She raised her eyes to Eden. "Do you understand? She doesn't want to be found."

"But why?"

"She told me she was going to run away to be with someone. Life at the lodge was impossible. Anyway, she didn't say who it was."

"Can we go somewhere to talk?"

They walked downstairs. Scooter was in a corner, his dance steps a delicate shuffle below the thickening body. He glanced her way and shouted, "Hey, Eden, looking good." His face spread in a glistening smile, the gold stud glowing in his ear, a bracelet flashing on his wrist. His feet kept moving, the cowboy hat firmly on his head.

Eden found herself pushed by the crowd along with Kathy to a place near the porch. It was quieter than elsewhere in the room. Kathy rested her head with her back against the wall, her eyes staring at the sea of sweaty faces and bobbing heads. Eden couldn't say what prompted her to ask, "So were you and Jess both teen moms around the same time?"

Kathy stared at her in silence. "She fell for a guy from the lodge."

"An employee or a visitor?"

"She wouldn't tell me."

Kathy told Eden how she and Jess helped each other pick out clothes to disguise their pregnancies. "She was good with clothes, and it worked for her and for me, too, for a while. We were able to fool people. She had an ability to find these old-fashioned outfits. They hid everything, and on her they looked cool."

"It's hard to imagine any woman being able to hide a pregnancy."

"I lived it for a while, she lived it, and if you go online, you'll find stories of women who were pregnant, and nobody could tell from their appearance. Jess was able to disguise it in all the old-fashioned stuff she wore. I wasn't able to keep my being pregnant a secret except for a short time. I figured Scooter would be furious, but it turns out he's great with Angela, a good uncle."

"What became of Jess's baby?"

"Probably adopted right after birth," Kathy said, "but we drifted apart, and when I saw her again, she wouldn't talk about it. Then she ran off."

"Running away. How can you be so sure?"

In the porch light Eden saw an uncharacteristically nervous expression on Kathy's face. "Haven't I told you enough? She said she was going to, and she did." She pushed off from the wall.

"Look, I need to see to my guests, sweetie," She slipped into the crowd.

Eden considered why Kathy wanted her to believe Jess had run away. She was crossing Kathy's front yard when one possibility came to her: if Eden kept asking around and pursuing Jess's disappearance, she might get results, and Angela might not see her father except during visiting hours in prison. Because Eden was certain she knew Angela's father. She'd seen Johnny reflected in the child's smile.

Then too, if Kathy could wield a gun or a knife as well as she could a hairdryer, Kathy might wind up in prison for having ended Jess's life in a jealous rage over Johnny's love for her and refusal to marry Kathy. No question but either way, Kathy would fight to protect her daughter. Eden admired her for this.

Like her brother, Scooter, Kathy had tried to deflect her attention from any possibility other than Jess running away. Eden wondered if between Kathy and Scooter there was a conspiracy to protect a business enterprise Jess might have threatened to expose. It was possible to buy and sell more than hair products at the stylish salon. Still, she had no evidence.

She decided she needed to think beyond the usual motives of greed, passion, and jealousy.

She was close to the road when she saw a woman at the foot of the path leading to Kathy's house. A large dog walked at her side. The woman ditched her cigarette, snuffing it out with her sandal. She opened the mailbox flap, ordering the dog to sit as she checked for bills and letters. The dog stood where it was, panting and gazing toward Eden, who realized the woman hadn't recognized her.

"Hey, Meg. When are we going to dive at Red Parker's Reef?"

Meg closed the mailbox flap. "I've been thinking about you and about the reef." Eden knew she was probably lying, but it was a small social lie of the kind people will often tell to keep things moving along smoothly. She was more interested in what she'd say next. "How about we go Saturday?" Meg said.

Eden walked over to her. The dog was delighted to meet Eden. While Eden patted the dog and bent down to let it lick her face, Meg named a time. She had equipment Eden could borrow.

"I'll see you at the marina," Eden called to Meg's retreating back. Meg pulled on the leash. The dog went with her into Kathy's house.

With Jess in her life, Meg had a family. With Jess gone, she'd found another.

She was walking north along the road when a white van pulled up, its window whirring open. "Hey, Eddie, want to get something to eat? I'm starved."

"Where'd you go? I looked for you." She had always been looking for him, even when she and Ted had married at the courthouse. She'd looked, hoping to see him, but Johnny wasn't there. "I couldn't find you," she said.

"Kathy's was too crowded. Too noisy. And too hot. I drove to the dunes," Johnny said, not meeting Eden's gaze. She wondered if he'd been with someone else.

Eden made a quick decision to hold off starting a conversation with Johnny about Angela. She was certain she already knew the answer about the identity of the child's father, though there was always the chance she was wrong.

There would be a right time to talk with him about Kathy and Angela. A right time for Eden to think about him being the father of a child whose mother suspected he had murdered Jess.

There was the low rumble of thunder and flicker of lightning to the west. She thought of Jess and Luke and Johnny, all of them together at the dunes. They used to race down to the sea, the surf reaching out to touch their naked bodies. Eden longed for this lost season. She climbed into the van. Johnny stepped on the accelerator.

Chapter Twenty-five

Eden used the bathroom and waited at the front door while Johnny searched for his credit card. Outside, a sudden storm with pounding rain and high wind sent branches crashing to the ground and trash flowing in the streets. The storm would last a short while. It would leave behind a steaming swamp. And lots of mosquitoes.

"Let's not go yet, Eddie." He walked from the kitchen, in his hands a bag of chips and a bottle of wine.

They sat in the living room on a hard couch. It was covered with a thin blanket to hide the torn places. Johnny poured wine from the bottle into plastic cups. He handed her one. There was a long crack in the patio door glass. Rain leaked around the edges of the masking tape.

"This place is like a home with you here, Eddie."

His expression was solemn, and she knew she needed to say something. But she felt rainy inside, the definition of who she was lost to her the way rain blurs the shape of things. Finally, it came to her.

"I'm not a homemaker, Johnny." Telling him this wasn't what he wanted from her, but it was true.

Holding his wine cup between his hands, Johnny bowed his head, then looked sideways at her. "We can do it together. We can find the right place for us; you need to give us a chance."

If she was going to bring up Angela, this could be a good time. But somewhere between the cups of wine, she stopped caring about anything except escaping from emptiness.

He lifted her from the couch and carried her to his bed. They twisted their arms and legs together, wrestling and laughing like kids. He stretched his full length on top of her. They gazed into each other's eyes, and there was a lot of fumbling with zippers and buttons.

Afterward, Eden rolled out from under his weight and went into the bathroom. There was a lingering taste of wine and plastic in her mouth. She had finished washing her hands and using his toothpaste when she heard her phone buzz. She walked into the bedroom and took the phone from a pocket of her discarded jeans. The call was from a local number. She didn't recognize it, but she answered.

"I want to speak to Eden." She thought it was a crank call and was tempted to end it without saying anything. But she thought she recognized the voice.

"Speaking."

"Do you remember me?"

"A name would help."

"Wanda."

She'd sat next to her on the bus from Chicago. She had met her again at Harbor Place.

"Is there something I can help you with, Wanda?" But make it snappy, Eden was thinking, and she realized her voice conveyed her impatience.

"I'm calling because I heard there was some guy around here who'd mentioned the name Jess. It's a common name and it's probably not the Jess Sinclair you're looking for information about, but I'm trying to find out when or what was said and who said it. I wanted to make sure I could reach you in case I pin anything down." Her voice was distant, like she was holding the phone away from her face, as if she feared the slap of rejection.

Eden said, "I appreciate it." She suspected Wanda may have made up the story of hearing Jess's name to have someone to chat with. The next thing Wanda said confirmed it.

"I got a job."

"Oh? Doing what?" Eden decided to talk to her for another minute, no more, and then she'd end the call. And program her phone to block the number Wanda had used. This wouldn't stop the girl from calling from another phone, but she might not be eager to try Eden again if she understood the earlier number had been put on a banned list. Wanda wasn't going to turn up anything about Jess. But neither had Eden.

"I keep the salon clean. I do shampoos sometimes when they get real busy."

"This is great news. Congratulations."

Johnny was stretched out on the bed with his arms folded behind his head. He glanced at her, then stared at the ceiling. He had departed emotionally from her. Eden ignored him and went on listening to Wanda.

"I'm taking the Greyhound to Chicago."

"You have a job, so naturally you're leaving?"

"This isn't where I want to be."

She should end the conversation and go to Johnny. But Wanda was talking about going home, a subject she wanted to hear more about. If they were going to be together, Johnny would need to learn to be understanding and patient.

"But Wanda, most everyone wants to be in Florida."

"It's too hot and damp, and the insect life is scary. I'm going to the Midwest."

"Chicago has such great weather. And no insects."

Wanda laughed.

"It's home."

Eden had no idea where home was. It hit her then, how much she was the one needing a friend, how empty she felt. She suspected if she stood out in the rain, letting it strike her, it would make the same echoing sound it was making as it hit the metal downspouts outside Johnny's apartment.

When Eden didn't say anything, Wanda said, "I have to go. I'll call again if I find out something."

Eden didn't believe Wanda would come up with anything more, but there was always a chance. She said, "You can call anytime." She wasn't going to program her phone after all.

"Thanks." There was a slight smile in Wanda's voice.

Eden stepped into her jeans and slipped the phone into a pocket. Johnny got up off the bed. He pulled her to him.

"When you're ready, you'll call me, and I'll come for you. We'll follow wherever the road takes us until we find our home, Eddie. It could be we'll settle in the mountains or near the ocean. I want you on my side and by my side," he said.

Eden was silent. Thoughts of Jess and her baby, of Kathy and Angela, questions of where home was, doubts about Johnny, these pressed against her heart. She had nothing to give him.

"Well?" Johnny said.

"I need you to take me to the lodge," Eden said.

He slammed a fist into his open palm.

She finished dressing and walked into the living room. She stood beside a window and listened to the slow withdrawal of the rain. It was the sound of endings.

She walked to the front door and opened it.

The apartment faced the street. Across from it a row of trash carts and cartons had been stacked outside the back doors of small businesses. Whatever the businesses were, they involved lots of boxes, mostly wet and collapsing.

A stray cat ran out from behind the carts and cartons. The cat pounced on something in the grass near Johnny's van. Eden hoped the stray had a warm dry place to curl up in, some place where it would be safe. She knew it was more likely it would roam all night, wet, afraid, and hungry.

She stepped outside and waited for him beside the van, Johnny shutting the apartment door with a hard sound. He walked toward her. In the moon's sharp blue glare, the hand he set on the passenger door was that of a stranger. She rode in silence beside him to the lodge. She might as well have been alone.

Chapter Twenty-six

She descended through shafts of strong morning sunlight in the water, her breathing making a soft, bubbling sound. Schools of fish flashed by. Meg was ahead of her. She'd brought photo equipment along.

Earlier, before loading their diving gear in the boat to the reef, Meg, scanning the cloudless sky, had asked Eden if she was sure she wanted to dive at Red Parker's. "The weather's changeable. And you're inexperienced," Meg said, "plus I only have really old equipment. If we put it off, though, we might not be able to get together again, at least not anytime soon."

"Waiting won't make me any more experienced. And it was Jess's favorite place," Eden said. "I want to go." She was not about to change her mind and miss the opportunity.

The wreck, ten miles from shore and seventy-five feet down, had tipped to one side, but its propeller and wings were intact. As she drew near, Eden felt Jess's presence.

She pictured her swimming above a wing, sitting in the cockpit, her red hair streaming. She imagined their grandfather, CJ, telling her and Jess about airplanes like the one ahead of her: *The Chance Vought F4U Corsair saw duty in World War II and Korea, mostly with the Marines. One day you girls could fly your own planes.*

In the distance, beyond the body of the Corsair, the prow of a military shipwreck loomed. Meg gestured her plan to photograph the Corsair, and then they'd visit the shipwreck. She switched on her photo light, and the aircraft, encrusted with sea life, bloomed with color.

She stayed close to Meg, watching her photograph schools of fish as they moved over the aircraft. The two divers went from one end of the airplane to the other, Eden gamely posing for multiple shots. After a while, but with Meg still nearby, she moved off to get a closer look at the cockpit.

In the drifting sand in the cockpit, something glittered. Next to it, a fragment of something white rested. Eden was about to thrust her hand toward the brightness when Meg appeared at her side. She pointed to herself, pointed at the distant shipwreck, and gestured for Eden to follow her there.

Eden understood Meg was ready to move on to take more photos, and she made a circle with her index finger and thumb to signal her okay. Then she turned to the airplane, to where the brightness had been.

But she was unable to touch whatever it was she had seen. It had been covered over in the shifting sand. Or carried away in the surging movement of water. With a last look at the Corsair, she followed Meg.

It had been gradual, but as she swam after Meg she noticed she was breathing harder from the effort to keep the young woman in sight. It was the current. It was becoming stronger by the minute. The water was growing dark. Clouds must be gathering. The shipwreck was far away.

Her dive teacher in Illinois would be proud of her for making wreck dives. She mentally reviewed the checklist of his lessons. She realized she hadn't kept track of her air supply. What she saw next told her she would need to surface within a few minutes. She slowed her breathing to conserve air.

Where was Meg? In the moments she had taken to check her air supply, she had lost sight of her. In the distance, the military wreck was rapidly vanishing like a ghost ship in a fog.

She looked around and above, finally glimpsing Meg off to the left as she emerged from the growing darkness. But the minutes lost waiting for Meg to show up had cost her; Eden's air supply was running dangerously low.

As Meg drew near, Eden brought her right hand to her heart, indicating to Meg she was low on air, and she gave the thumbs-up sign signaling her intention to surface. Meg tapped the regulator in her mouth, inviting Eden to buddy breathe.

Eden had practiced life-saving air-sharing techniques in a swimming pool with her instructor. But something in the way Meg waved for her to come in close convinced her she would have to risk getting to the surface entirely on her own.

Or she would never make it there alive.

Eden gave the thumbs-up sign once more and began to work her way slowly to the surface. She forced herself to breathe slowly. She forced herself not to panic.

She ascended into deep rolling swells, dark skies, and the welcome sight of another boat. Two men sporting dive gear, close-cropped haircuts, massive muscles, and bristling with spear guns helped her aboard. Meg followed and the men took them to where they'd left their boat anchored at the Corsair. There was less than a minute's air supply left in her tank.

Heavy squalls hit, the men aborted their own dive, and Eden and Meg followed them to the marina. It was a rough trip back, but Eden knew she'd survived a far worse fate than being bounced around by the waves. She remembered what people said about flying: any flight you walked away from was a good one. The same could be said of diving. This had been a good dive; she was going to walk away from it.

She took a deep breath of salty air. As the boat neared the marina, Kitty's words came to her: *don't trust anyone.* She turned her gaze behind her, toward Red Parker's Reef, her thoughts on lost glittery things and the whiteness of shell. Or bone.

Chapter Twenty-seven

Cap yelled into the phone, "You better get over here for a sit-down with your aunt and me." Eden was tempted not to show up. On second thought she decided being a no-show would be cowardly. It was better to confirm her suspicions as to what it was all about.

Aunt Billie and Cap were waiting, poised on the edge of their chairs inside his cabin at the dining room table. They did not offer her whatever awful thing it was they were drinking, which appeared to involve assorted exotic liquors mixed with fruit juices. They did not ask her to sit down. She knew what they were going to say.

She said, "Hey, Aunt Billie, hey, Cap. Good to see you both even though you're about to fire me."

Two pairs of eyes widened.

"Let me just say that firing me would be bad for business." If they challenged her on this point, she would mention the thousands of dollars she had saved them by working unpaid. "I'm a valuable asset," she said.

Cap spoke first. He didn't address what Eden had said. He had his little speech and he spit it out.

"What you told your aunt about me scheming to sell the lodge behind her back is a complete and total lie. A document I'd prepared for her with all the information describing an unexpected opportunity for us to make money was unfortunately misplaced."

"What a shocker."

Cap's face was trending toward purple. "She has been told what's happening and fully approves of everything I've been trying to do for her. For us." He considered his hands folded prayer-like before him on the table. Eden doubted he was praying even though he had good reason to do so. She decided a higher power would be sorely pressed to forgive his lies.

Aunt Billie's brightly colored lips straining to appear happy revealed misery. Her gaze wandered around the room as though it was unfamiliar to her. She hadn't been to Cap's former love nest in a long while. Cap sprang from his chair and whisked Aunt Billie's empty glass off the table. "Hold on, be right back." He disappeared into the kitchen.

Eden said, "So when is the closing on the lodge?"

Aunt Billie snapped a glance over her shoulder, looking for Cap. He was talking on his phone. She helped herself to something thick and green and drank it down.

"Him and me are partners," she said. "Always have been since first we laid eyes on each other at a beer fest right here at the lodge."

Cap had returned with a glass full of whiskey and a cherry sunk in its amber depths. He set it beside Aunt Billie, who started on the whiskey after eating the cherry.

"He's wanting to get the best deal possible for us. He's studying up and talking to folks. We've decided our future together doesn't include this old dump." Aunt Billie reached out to squeeze his hand. He snatched his hand out of reach.

The lodge was going to be sold soon, against what CJ, Luke, and Jess would've wished. She wondered where Ruth would go. This had been her home from the time anyone could remember.

Cap thrust a finger at her. He said, "You told your aunt I never served our glorious country. I was sent on numerous risky and highly classified missions. Information about me and how I saved my nation can never be revealed. We are done helping you."

His mad eyes burned into her chest. He had to be a master at lying having gotten away with it for many years, and she wondered if he'd been so good at it he'd fooled himself and come to believe his own lies.

Aunt Billie took a wheezing breath. "You have gone and meddled with what Cap and me have together. Let me tell you we do not appreciate it. You nearly ruined everything we have worked so hard to build. And here we have generously helped you out in your time of need. You can go get your things, Eden. You are officially no longer employed here."

It might have been amusing but not enlightening to prolong the meeting by arguing with them. She had sensed it was coming, and she'd braced herself. Still, it felt as though Cap and Aunt Billie had pushed her to the floor and taken turns kicking her. She told herself she was not going to let them break her.

Upstairs in Jess's room she folded the few clothes she'd brought to the lodge. She removed the papers from the secret compartment, and she set the clothes and papers in her backpack and walked down the stairs. It was most likely for the last time.

She glanced over her right shoulder into the hallway below in the direction of Ruth's rooms. She didn't see any lights. Ruth and Raynell had probably gone out or were watching television, and Eden did not want to disturb them. Ruth might lose her job if she involved herself with Eden. She would call her, once she figured out what to do next.

Downstairs she saw a light under the door at Bobby Hayes's room off the south porch. He'd given her another tip, and he might try to help her, but it wouldn't be right to involve a guest in her troubles. She left by the east porch, crossed the road, and headed to the beach.

The sound of a guitar came to her from the sea and from the rustling sea oats growing on the dunes. The sound took her to a small group of people. She quickly learned their names. Leah and Suzy, Rick and his dog, Buster. The guitar and Buster had traveled with Rick from California, up the coast to Oregon, and on into Alaska. Then to the heartland and east with the rising sun. Leah and Suzy had met him at Harbor Place.

Tomorrow he'd hop a train, he told them, and head west again. He'd jump off with Buster "when we can see wide open plains and sky, some mountains in the distance." The little group had been drawn together by Rick's music.

Leah, noticing Eden's sadness, told her if she let the music enter her heart it would comfort her. Suzy nodded agreement. Eden asked if they had heard the name Jess Sinclair? Jess was a common name, but they shook their heads no. She told them her cousin's story, hoping they'd recognize something about her from the details.

Leah said, "Someone was talking about a hotel going in where another one burned down and a girl went missing. Someone said they found an old purse around there a few days ago."

They all looked at Leah, the expectation being she might say more to connect what she'd said with Eden's story of her cousin. Seeing their stares, Leah said, "I thought I'd mention it. Another missing girl."

Eden glanced along the coast. She imagined ribbons of light from a giant Ferris wheel turning against the night sky, the smell of popcorn, the sounds of music and laughter, crowds of people roaming a boardwalk.

And she heard screams of people fleeing the Golden Cove fire.

Beyond the slope of the dunes, there were houses furnished with big beds covered in cool sheets on firm mattresses. Tonight, Eden's new friends would drift to sleep in the doorways of supermarkets, drugstores, the library. It was clear and warm tonight. The weeds would make fragrant beds. But she knew they would not be safe.

Eden had a bed to sleep in unless the rattler came back to claim it. She could always walk the long miles to the Blue Moon. She had a friend there.

She left the little group and followed a path in the forest parallel to the lodge driveway, the trees, vines, the long-leaved splashes of tropical plants and ferns giving her cover. At the sound of vehicles behind her, she pressed herself flat on the ground. It was Cap's Chevy. A van followed it with a South Carolina license plate. They continued to Cap's. She would not bother to see what they were up to.

Eden got off the ground, her clothes leafy and damp, and she walked around the north end of the lodge and made her way to CJ's cabin. Its kitchen door was unlocked. Inside, she checked the rooms, using her phone flashlight.

In the bathroom she hesitated before lifting the closed toilet lid. She raised it and stepped back. It looked like a nest of snakes in there. It was stains. Nothing jumped at her from the commode.

She went into the hallway and stood still, listening. If there was another presence, she thought she would sense a smell or hear a sound indicating she had company. She thought about the spider in CJ's hidden storage compartment. She hoped it would remain in its web.

In a cupboard in the kitchen, she found stale crackers and a can of chili. She ate, too hungry to bother heating the food, and then she called Johnny. She couldn't reach him, his voicemail was full, and there was more to tell him than she had patience to type into a text message. She sent a short one asking him to call.

She'd wait before trying to reach Ruth. There was one other person she found herself thinking of. She was prepared to hear he wasn't available.

He answered her call. From the background noise of announcers' voices and the roar of a crowd together with closer sounds of conversation and the clink of glasses, it sounded as though he was at a bar watching a sports event on television. Eden wouldn't mind being there with him, especially if the place offered food and McCabe was buying. The chili had been good, even cold, but she would never turn down a free meal.

Chapter Twenty-eight

The moon was 238,900 miles away. It was shaped like a cat's claw. There was a second moon Eden knew about. It was much closer to earth, and it was bright blue and full. She gripped her hands together in her lap and looked out the airplane's window. Concentrating on this second moon helped calm her. There had been many times she'd wished the wind would carry the Blue Moon and its sign to some other planet.

But as the airplane moved through the night, she thought of the trailer park as a refuge. Annie would never be there again, but Eden would visit with Kitty, and when he learned she was there, Ted would come over, and they'd talk. About what she wasn't sure. She hoped things would go well between them, and they could part as friends. She shut her eyes, willing the plane onward. The control tower chatter out of Jacksonville faded. She woke up when a male voice spoke loud in her ear. "Rise and shine, Eden. We're about to land." Her eyes flew open.

McCabe, in his watch cap, glanced at her from the controls of a Cessna single-engine light plane. When she called him from CJ's cabin, she hadn't had the chance to tell him she had been fired from her job before McCabe was saying he was about to fly north for an unplanned assignment, and he invited her to go with him. He did not offer details of the work he was to do, nor did she ask.

"Your hometown will be less than an hour from where I'm going. Are you interested in a ride?" he'd asked. "It'll be a quick trip."

Immediately, Eden's hands began to sweat, and her stomach churned. Both CJ and Luke had been pilots, and she admired them. But when the possibility of flying was presented to her, she hadn't been sure this was something she wanted to do. She'd never been in an airplane. From somewhere in the shadows of CJ's cabin, she heard Luke gently chiding her to develop an adventurer's spirit. She did not want to let him down.

Still, McCabe was a mystery. He disappeared from her life for days and never talked about where he went or what he did. He said he knew Luke, but she wondered how well and whether the picture with Luke might have been doctored. There was the photo of the woman and baby. And they'd be flying at night. Still, even with all her discomfort, making the trip with McCabe was tempting.

"I don't have the money," she'd told McCabe earlier.

"It's not required."

"It's free?"

"I didn't say it was free."

So far he'd never set a hand on her.

By the time they landed, and she climbed in the rental car he'd arranged for her, he still had not explained anything about the trip costs.

"So how am I to repay you?" she said as she slid behind the steering wheel.

"You're going to fly us back to Jax," he said, easing the car door closed.

"Do you have a death wish, McCabe?"

He ignored her comment. "You're going to find out how easy flying is. Then you'll get your pilot's license."

"Flying lessons involve money I don't have."

"You see the plane over there?" He nodded toward the Cessna. "The airplane belongs to me. Learning to fly is the price of this trip." He closed the car door and walked away.

Eden took the interstate west. Soon skyscrapers gave way to endless fields with soil so rich it was black. Raynell would want to take pictures here of fields at dawn and at sunset, fields churning with wind and resting beneath a light dusting of snow.

Spending the summer in Florida had given Eden a new appreciation of winter.

She exited the interstate, slowing on a country road. It took her by modest homes where gardens overflowed with flowers and vegetables. She hadn't realized it before, but she was homesick for this little town.

After debating whether to call Kitty to tell her of the spur-of-the-moment trip, Eden settled on surprising her friend in person. The sun was beginning to show brown and orange at the horizon. It was too early to knock on Kitty's door.

Eden parked out in front of 1840 Blue Moon Boulevard, the grand name for the unpaved and rutted road where she lived. Trailer-park humor. As she inserted a key in the lock, something made her glance to one side before stepping across the threshold. The hood of a car was visible from where it was parked around the back. She knew who it belonged to.

She doubted his love for her had made him sense she was on her way and had sent him hurrying over. But she thought it possible he had decided to move in again. He hadn't gotten around to telling her. She opened the door and went in. She called his name.

Two figures stumbled from the bedroom. One of them wore jockey shorts. He wiped sleep from his eyes. The woman with him wore bikini underpants. She clung to his side.

"Oh, wow," Ted said.

"O-M-G, this is not happening," the girl said. She was far more articulate than Ted.

The girl headed into the back bedroom and reemerged in a man's shirt. It fell to her fat little knees.

Eden recognized it as one of Ted's shirts having washed it many times. Ted had pulled on a shirt, too. They were both at least partly clad, which was to Eden a small mercy. More of their clothes were in a heap in front of the television where passion had evidently overtaken them.

"Hello, Ted. Please leave at once."

"Let me explain. Can't I explain?"

"I am sorry, but no, you cannot explain. I have important work to do."

Eden stood at the door with her arms folded like armor across her chest. Ted and his girlfriend hustled into their jeans.

Ted touched her shoulder on his way out the door. "I'll call later," he said in a flirtatious voice. He smelled garlicky.

"Don't bother."

"Does this mean you're going to divorce me?" He sounded eager.

"I'm not sure," Eden said. She knew it was beneath her not to be straight with him, but still it felt good for the moment. "But probably yes," she relented.

She stood in the doorway watching Ted and his girlfriend drive away. Then she wandered around, inspecting. They'd left behind revolting slices of cold pizza and dirty sheets.

Eden threw the pizza along with the sheets into a garbage cart. She thought better about the pizza, retrieved it, and scattered torn pieces for the wild critters living in the woods. They were always hungry.

She stood next to the cart watching the sun rise. It was beautiful. She didn't need anything more.

But this wasn't so. She needed to find Jess, and if she was going to, she had to hustle and get back to the lodge. If she was careful, she could continue to live at CJ's indefinitely. As she started looking for mail next to the dead cactus Kitty had mentioned, McCabe called.

"This is a reminder not to lose track of the time," McCabe said.

"I'm searching for some mail."

"I can drive out there and search with you. I'm about a half-hour away." He sounded like he was right next-door. "You need to be thorough and meticulous. I can give you guidance."

"Thanks for the offer, but I have to go. I spotted a dead cactus."

"Cactus?" This was followed by silence.

"You'd have to have spent time with my mom to appreciate this as a positive development for finding what I'm looking for, although obviously it's way too late for the cactus to benefit."

"Give it water."

"I appreciate your instructions in the finer points of gardening."

"Anytime. You're flying us back to Jax. Don't forget."

"There's a career for you in comedy clubs."

The cactus was on a table. The table had a fourth leg consisting of an unsteady stack of books. Eden gave the shriveled plant water and spoke a few encouraging words over it. She liked cacti. She settled in an armchair with its stuffing coming out and began to read.

The mail included opened and unopened letters. The first thing she read was a letter from Cap telling Annie to sign an enclosed form transferring her name from one company to another with a different name. Cap said CJ wanted her do this. The letter didn't say what the companies did but it warned if she didn't sign she'd lose the money he claimed to have persuaded CJ to leave her. Cap didn't specify the amount.

Money going to Annie from CJ was news to Eden. Because the letter was from Cap, she found it suspect, and she wondered what Annie had thought of it and if she had signed the form and mailed it back.

The letter from Cap was dated a month before Annie's death in April. Eden and Ted had been living in an apartment then, but she saw Annie every day, and Annie had never told her of the letter from Cap. Annie might not have mentioned it under any circumstances. She was as secretive as CJ. The form she was to sign was no longer with the letter.

In the best of times Annie was disorganized, and she had been frail to the point of being skeletal by the time the letter had reached her. Eden thought it over and decided Annie, too exhausted to deal with the complexities of stamps and addresses, might have placed the form in one of the locations she used for filing.

There were several other pieces of mail. Mostly advertisements. Eden sorted through them, nearly overlooking the envelope postmarked with a date not long before Annie had died. She opened the envelope and removed the letter inside.

The letter was in CJ's cramped handwriting, made more difficult to read from ink smears and blotches. Still, she understood CJ was leaving Annie a sizeable inheritance. With his last sentence, he told Annie he loved her. Annie had died never learning this from her father. The envelope had been sealed until Eden opened it.

She got up out of the chair and began to search for the form Cap's letter had directed Annie to sign. The search took her to the places Annie used for her filing system: the top of the refrigerator in an empty cereal box, beneath a certain frying pan in the oven's warming drawer, the inside of the oven itself, under a mattress, behind a roll of food wrap, under a stack of dishes, inside a cracker box. When she reached beneath a pile of sweaters in a drawer, soft paper yielded to her touch.

It was a package wrapped in tissue paper. Eden finished pulling the package from the drawer and opened it. Inside was an infant's dress embroidered with the letter "J." Pinned to the dress was a message in Annie's writing: "Billie, please accept this. Thank you."

It had to be a gift she intended to send to Billie, her estranged sister, meant for Jess. Eden returned the package to the drawer and continued to search without turning up the missing form. Annie had reached out to Billie at least once. Nothing she'd ever heard from Billie suggested her aunt had ever done the same.

The sun's rays were coming through the blinds. Eden glanced at her phone's clock. The time she had agreed to meet McCabe was rapidly approaching, and she closed the trailer and walked to Kitty's place. She knocked.

A curtain stirred at the window. Suddenly there was Kitty standing inside the doorway in the shadows. She wore a flowered housecoat and fluffy turquoise bunny slippers.

"You should've told me you were coming. What if I had missed you? Oh, honey, I'd have cried my eyes out with hurt. You should have called. It wouldn't have mattered what time it was."

Eden followed her friend inside. Over a plate of banana chocolate muffins and a mug of coffee she filled her in on what had been happening in her life.

Then Kitty shared some news.

"The Blue Moon will be gone by the end of summer. It's a good thing you're here to pack up things." Something in Eden's expression prompted what she asked next. "You are staying, aren't you?"

"Kitty, I'm going to the lodge again soon. I can't give up searching for answers about Jess."

"But you will be back, won't you? My new boyfriend, the policeman, has a second job with a moving company. He will help you. There's lots of storage units available. People have too many things."

"I'll probably toss most of Annie's belongings." It felt like she was betraying Annie. But storage units came with a monthly rental she could not afford.

Kitty nodded and patted her hand.

The sun was up as Kitty saw Eden to the door. In the room's shadows and with the heavy makeup Kitty wore, Eden hadn't seen what the strong morning light revealed. The flesh around Kitty's eye still showed faint bruises. She studied Kitty's face and found other marks of violence.

As Eden studied her, Kitty's eyes welled with tears. Eden said, "If I could, I'd kill the monster who did this," and she held her friend close.

Kitty said, "Come home soon." Not for the first time, Eden wondered where home was. She thought it might have something to do with having a friend like Kitty. Even if she lived on a couch in this trailer, being with Kitty would make it home.

Eden stepped into her rental car as Kitty waved a tearful farewell.

McCabe waited for her at the Cessna.

"You're going to take off and land the aircraft. I think you'll find it's exciting."

And she did.

McCabe let her nap in between.

Chapter Twenty-nine

Around 4 a.m. the smell of smoke reaching Eden while she slept at CJ's cabin sent her hurrying through the wilderness to the lodge. On the south porch, Ruth and Raynell were taking turns sharing field glasses with Bobby Hayes. They were gazing at the flames shooting from the roof of Cap's cabin. Eden was concealed by vines and bushes, and they did not see her. The flames spread an eerie glow on Cap's Chevy and motorcycle parked at the cabin. The wail of fire engines floated in the air as Eden ran to his place and went into the burning building through the kitchen. Her shouts were greeted by the roar of the flames. To her left in his study and gunroom behind veils of smoke, a woman leaned forward in a chair with her head and shoulders bowed over Cap's desk. There were shot glasses and bottles of whiskey and brandy on the desktop. Cap's vintage P38 pistol rested nearby.

"Aunt Billie?" Eden stepped toward her. Aunt Billie slowly raised her head, Eden gasping at the sight of her ruined face. It was flecked with vomit and blood.

"I killed the bastard," Aunt Billie rasped. Blood seeped from at least two wounds in her face and neck. There were more wounds. Her clothes were soaked with blood.

"You shot Cap?" She moved closer.

There was a long rattling sigh, her arm sweeping the bottles, glasses, and weapon off the desk as she attempted to grab Eden before sliding from the chair onto the floor.

Eden struggled to breathe as rolls of heavy smoke engulfed the room. She glimpsed a wooden box on the desk, but she could not reach it. She was sinking down. From behind, someone seized her around the waist. It was the last thing she remembered.

She woke up at CJ's not recalling how she'd gotten there, but with the horrible memory of Aunt Billie's ravaged face glaring at her from inside the smoke. She threw off the dusty quilt and returned to the scene. Firemen were directing streams of water on the cabin from high-pressure hoses.

The cabin was a charred ruin, the air filled with smoke and ash. All traces of the animal trophies once covering the walls were gone, as if the animals had come alive and fled into the wilderness. The refrigerator was on its side, its doors open. Eden didn't see Cap's frozen fish anywhere. The coolers were no longer around, either. She recognized a tall blond woman in a police uniform and started toward her. Someone else reached Officer Campbell before she could, and Eden hung back.

"Where have you been? I've been worried you'd disappeared like Jess did."

"I guess you didn't get my messages," Eden said, "about being fired and going to Chicago. Ruth, you might have lost your job if you'd gotten involved."

Ruth's eyes glowed with anger. "I will try to understand what you've told me. You were fired and all you do is leave me a voicemail?" She shook her head, her face softening. "You can tell me some other time how you got to Chicago and back so quick. You must've sprouted some powerful wings."

"I think Aunt Billie's dead or close to it," Eden said. "I found her in the cabin."

"And yesterday she was talking about all the money Cap had promised she'd get by selling the lodge." Ruth was plainly neither surprised nor saddened at the news. There had always been a coolness between her and Billie.

"Where's Cap?"

"I haven't seen him. Aunt Billie said she'd killed him. She had a gun."

247

Eden glanced into the small crowd and found Officer Campbell. Their eyes met. Eden walked over to her. She gave the officer a statement about finding her aunt with a P38 and what might have been her final words about killing Cap.

Eden and Ruth watched as a loaded stretcher was carried toward an ambulance. Ruth turned to Eden and said, "Don't you go disappearing on me anymore. It was about this time of the year, in August, when we lost Jess."

Though the early morning was humid and hot, Ruth pulled a sweater around her narrow shoulders. Eden watched as the older woman followed the forest path to the lodge, trails of smoke rising around her like offerings.

Ruth hadn't been gone long before a shape appeared near the edge of the woods. It surveyed the still smoldering ruins from wild yellow eyes. Then the fox vanished into the wilderness.

***

Later in the morning, Eden watched pictures roll across the television screen showing Aunt Billie in her beauty pageant crown and sash followed by pictures from the past of Cap sitting on his Harley and Johnny standing on the lodge east porch steps, his thumbs hooked through the belt loops of his jeans. There were pictures of the smoking remains of the cabin and an exterior shot of the lodge. It had not been damaged in the fire. But it looked decayed and forlorn. The broadcast offered details of the lives involved:

"The lifeless body of Belinda 'Billie' Sinclair, 61, entertainment manager at the Fox Dunes Lodge and a former beauty queen, was found in the predawn hours today inside a burning cabin on lodge grounds in Magnolia Beach. The cabin's lone tenant, Captain George "Cap" Williams, a decorated war hero and prominent fundraiser for vet programs, is believed to have been wounded in the incident and is missing. The police are seeking handyman Johnny Bright for questioning. Arson is suspected. The lodge was built by the recently deceased Ms. Sinclair's father, the late CJ Sinclair."

Aunt Billie had been pronounced dead at the scene from multiple gunshot wounds, most but not all of Cap's weapons collection appeared to have been stolen, and the cabin was a total loss. Broadcasters reported this was not the first time tragedy had struck what they described as "the prominent beach family. Ms. Sinclair's daughter, Jess, went missing three years ago and her son, Luke, was killed while serving in Afghanistan."

The report included a news conference, reporters asking if there could be any connection between this latest tragedy and Jess Sinclair's disappearance. Officer Campbell said it was too early to make a determination. "I can tell you there is an active investigation into the Sinclair disappearance. We will be examining all aspects of both cases." Eden could hardly believe what she'd heard. The police were reopening Jess's case.

The questions at the press conference continued. Did the police have any leads on Cap Williams or Johnny Bright? Officer Campbell said several leads were being pursued, but she declined to say anything more. What about evidence of drugs at the scene?

"We have no further comment at this time." The press conference was wrapping up when someone shouted an apparently unrelated question about a purse dug up in the area of the Golden Cove Hotel and boardwalk fire. Officer Campbell said it was not part of her jurisdiction, but she added it was being sent for analysis.

Eden wanted to urge him to turn himself in. But before calling, she changed her mind and pocketed the instrument. He'd probably ditched his phone already to foil authorities tracing his whereabouts.

She jogged south along the road toward downtown. In the drainage ditch beside her, delicate ring patterns floated and vanished in the brown water. There was a lingering scent of smoke on her clothes and in the air. She knew it was remote at best, but there was always a chance she could catch Johnny at his apartment.

Eden took a left off the main road and turned in at the row of pastel-colored apartments where Johnny lived. The scent of a grilling steak left her feeling sick with longing for a dinner with someone who wanted her. It wouldn't matter if they drank wine from plastic cups or if the couch was covered with a blanket to hide the torn places. She pounded on his door and tried the handle. The door to Johnny's apartment swung open, heavy silence shuffling toward her like an old man.

A magazine story on camping was open on the scarred coffee table. Beige curtains were pulled partway across the busted patio door, where masking tape still managed to hold the glass together. The kitchen shelves and closets were empty, the bed stripped. In the refrigerator, half an avocado blossoming with mold offered a sign of life. It was disheartening to find herself searching for drugs and stolen guns, anything with blood on it. Mostly for signs of other women.

At the apartment next to Johnny's, a guy answered her knock. He stepped back as he finished pulling a shirt over his shaved sunburned head and shoving his arms through its sleeves. Music blasted from the living room. She asked him whether he'd seen or heard anything from his neighbor. He glowered at her.

"Look, lady, I don't have time for you or neighbors, I got to get to work," and he slammed the door. She knew about being underpaid and pushed around. Life was hard and then you died. And most of the time you were running on empty.

An unidentified caller was trying to reach her using a local area code. She answered. It might be Johnny. Or Wanda.

"Eddie, I can't talk long." He sounded like he was calling from the bottom of the ocean.

"What's going on? Are you okay?" There had to be something better to say, but there were no guidebooks addressing these circumstances.

"I didn't kill Miss Billie. I didn't torch Cap's place. I drove up, the place was burning, and it looked to me like if anyone was inside, they couldn't survive. I didn't go in. Then I heard I was being sought in the murder."

"You must give yourself up, Johnny. You've nothing to hide."

"I knew you'd say that." His voice was angry. Then pleading. "Eddie, there's nobody left who believes in me." His voice cracked. "Meet me and we'll run away together. I heard about a place down south near a river. We could fish and live off the land."

"You can't outrun the police."

"Listen, my prints are on every single one of Cap's guns from cleaning them."

"No, you listen to me, Johnny, you've got to tell me more about this and about Jess."

Eden stared at the dead phone in her hand, as though willing the instrument to spring to life so she could hear his voice again. So he would tell her something to make the hugeness of what was happening fit in the palm of her hand. Something to reduce the horror to a manageable size.

She followed the beach north toward the lodge, the memory of his voice weighing on her. As she ran, she pictured a boy coming toward her with a slow ragged smile, a stray with his ribs sticking out. She wanted to give him shelter.

Chapter Thirty

Storm clouds were building to the south in the late afternoon. The lake was glassy. On the far shore, a large white bird lifted from a tree and flew west. The wilderness smelled of smoke from the recent cabin fire, but there were no buzzards circling overhead, no sickly smell of rotting flesh. If she made any discoveries at the lake it wouldn't be because she'd found a body. She walked as far as the shoreline allowed before it turned into impenetrable jungle. Behind her a small dock jutted between thick cattails into the water. Near it, a weathered rowboat rested on the lake's sandy beach.

A slight ripple told her something was gliding along the muddy bottom of the lake. She knew what it might be, its legs stumbling over submerged branches, pushing aside the thick stems of water weeds, its thrashing tail dislodging rocks.

It surfaced, and she watched as water parted across its back and long snout. Soon after it lumbered out of the water, the grinning mouth showed off its fine necklace of teeth. It directed an unblinking stare at Eden.

From the surrounding trees, more long-legged white birds lifted their wings and flew away. Eden backed off, not taking her eyes from the scaly body. It was best to give the 'gator some space.

The alligator turned and launched itself into the water. It pointed its snout toward the middle of the lake and a small island there, sensing an opportunity for a meal it wouldn't have to struggle over the way it would if it decided on having Eden for dinner. Unwary fish or turtles were probably not going to live long enough to swim another day.

There was a rumble of thunder. The alligator sank in the lake, the surface of the water closing over it. The large white birds returned to settle like guardian ghosts in the trees. Standing where she was, she watched as the last rays of the sun gave her a fast-fading view of a narrow trail leading into the wilderness.

She was thinking about the night when Cap and Mitch had stood on the shore near Cap's place smoking dope, Cap pointing across the lake in the direction of the path she was looking at. She had a feeling about what she would find over there.

It was still illegal around these parts except for a handful of government-licensed growers. This was a good spot for an unauthorized patch. The alligators living in the lake might have given any unwary trespassers serious second thoughts about making the crossing to harvest marijuana plants.

The boat was the quickest way to get there. She and Jess along with Luke and Johnny used to take the boat out to explore.

Traces of rain touched her face.

Eden, deciding to test her skills, righted the rowboat. Its paddles were stowed underneath, and she launched it, jumped in, and pushed off as larger drops of rain began to fall. Mosquitoes were attacking in the moist air.

As she glided near the small island, she spotted two alligators in the weeds observing her from half-closed eyes. They were unconcerned by her presence, and she did not need to think about it for long to conclude why. She was outnumbered in alien territory. She had come close to forgetting this.

It was unclear to her what would happen when the police made a search and found the marijuana she was certain was growing in the forest. And a discovery was likely as they went about investigating Aunt Billie's murder and the disappearance of both Cap and Johnny. She wondered how far into the wilderness the weed farm extended. Proving it had anything to do with Jess's death might be hard.

The wind had picked up, ruffling the surface of the lake. A bolt of lightning hit the ground across the lake in the spot where she was headed, rain falling faster. It was time to consider whether searching for a patch of weed was worth it. Especially with its scaly guards watching her.

Eden let the boat drift. After a moment spent reviewing all options, she paddled to the dock.

From inside the weeds and cattails, from behind a curtain of rain, they were grinning. This was how she would prefer to think of the animals. The image of two men laughing over the body of an alligator lying pale and still in the moonlight would finally let her go.

Chapter Thirty-one

She was on her way to the beach, hauling the surfboard McCabe had left for her to practice with, when her phone buzzed. She propped the board against one of the stone posts at the lodge entrance and slipped the instrument from her shirt pocket. It wasn't like she had been counting the days. She wasn't even sure exactly when he had left, but her feeling was he'd been away for a longer time than he'd mentioned after the trip to Chicago and back.

"I want to tell you something important."

"You secretly work for a hostile foreign nation. You hijacked the airplane and you don't have a pilot's license. Go ahead. I'm listening."

"Luke and I got into a fight."

"With Luke, fighting was routine. What was it about?"

"Jess disappeared right around the time he shipped out, and Luke felt guilty and responsible, like he should have been there for her. He thought he could have prevented whatever happened to her. He'd been savagely blaming himself, and I pushed him over the edge."

"In what way? Luke was tough."

"I told him Jess was probably dead. Eden, I took away Luke's hope. And he hauled off and slugged me. We went a few rounds. I crashed into some glass. There's a scar on my forehead. I've kept it hidden because I knew you'd ask, and I would have had to tell you about the fight. Loyalty to your family might have made you stop seeing me."

"Why tell me now?"

"The other night on the way to Chicago you were sleeping, and I realized you deserved to hear what happened between me and Luke. I didn't want to conceal it from you. Make it seem like things were easy between us. They weren't. We respected each other."

There was silence. Then McCabe spoke.

"Eden, I am sorry."

"You had nothing to do with Jess, McCabe." Although he might have. In the fluid world of the beach community, McCabe could have met Jess while surfing, gone out with her, and murdered her.

Johnny claimed McCabe's name was familiar, but nothing about him so far put McCabe at Magnolia Beach and in Jess's company. Meg never mentioned anyone with his name. Neither had

Kathy or Scooter. But still, as Kitty had said, Eden should trust no one.

She asked McCabe, "Did you ever meet her?"

McCabe said, "Spending time with you, I have a better idea of what she was like. So I feel like I have met her. How's the surfing going?"

He was changing the subject. She wondered if it meant anything.

"Are you there, Eden?"

"Yeah. I'm making progress," she said.

"The ocean can be a dangerous place. So stay focused and alert, and stay safe."

"Yes, sir," Eden said. He was patronizing and bossy, but was he a murderer?

He asked her to join him for tamales. Eden agreed. She would go out with McCabe for the free meal but be wary.

She ended the call, grabbed the surfboard, and was about to start across the road when a red pickup approached. The guy at the wheel wore a dark watch cap. The girl beside him flipped long hair off her shoulders.

The red pickup zipped past, sand swirling in its wake, the blowback hot and metallic. After it had gone, Eden crossed the main road. She rested a minute before taking a sharp left turn. She carried the board all the way to the fox dunes pier.

She didn't need anyone.

Eden paddled out and straddled the board, facing the dunes. There was a guy sitting halfway up the big dune near the walkway. Both his arms rested across the tops of his knees. Instinct told her who it was.

"Johnny!" Eden caught a wave. It wasn't long before she toppled from the board. By the time she reached the place where she had seen Johnny, he was no longer there.

Johnny was on the run. She was angry with him for this. And she loved him still.

When she returned to the lodge, she found a stamped envelope waiting for her on the kitchen table. The envelope contained a sheet of paper with the message: "I cannot wait much longer for you. I shall have to consider my options." He wanted to frighten her.

Eden ripped up the latest from her devoted fan.

Chapter Thirty-two

One other car was at the funeral home when Eden pulled into its lot. She stepped out of Aunt Billie's Camry and walked inside. She set the pot of orchids she'd brought with her beside her aunt's coffin. She'd purchased the delicate flowers from a nursery earlier in the day. The broken one from her aunt's room was struggling to survive at the lodge. Eden was encouraging it to regrow.

An older man impeccably dressed in a dark suit, white shirt, and blue tie, stood near a wall. There was no one else in the room, and because of the way he was dressed, she thought he might have something official to do with the funeral home. But after introducing herself, she learned he was there to say farewell to Billie. His name was Joe Franklinson.

"We went out a few times in high school. I thought she was cute, but she drank too much and cried a lot. Too sensitive, I decided. Plus, she liked the biker types and hippies, so I never had a chance with her anyway. I'm an accountant."

Eden was tempted to tell Mr. Franklinson he was better off not having tried to form a meaningful bond with her aunt. But for all she knew, they might have made a solid couple. They might've helped each other spiritually, if Aunt Billie hadn't given her heart to a slimeball.

"Did you ever marry?"

"No," Mr. Franklinson said. "I guess I carried a torch for her all these years even with all her problems. But those scared me off. So here I am. I feel real bad, the way she died. It was awful. And then those kids of hers, they're gone, too."

Eden was silent. She was thinking of Jess's child. And Luke's heroism in saving lives on the battlefield. Both Jess and Luke had contributed to life. "Yes, it's sad they didn't live a whole lot longer."

She and Mr. Franklinson sat in folding metal chairs beside Aunt Billie's closed coffin. They were both silent. Eden forced herself to picture her aunt in her glory days as Miss Magnolia Beach, wearing a pretty dress and her sash and crown. She'd found the dress, sash, and crown while rummaging in her closet and decided Aunt Billie would have approved the choice for her burial.

Mr. Franklinson broke the silence. He was saying, "I went out there to see her at the lodge from time to time. I'm glad I have those memories.

There were square dances and cookouts, and it was nice."

Eden tried to think of good moments with Aunt Billie to share with him. She mentioned seeing pictures from the beauty pageant, and he agreed Aunt Billie had been "a looker who turned heads and could strut her stuff," as he put it.

"She made sure her guests always had something to eat and drink," Eden said. "She took care of them." It wasn't much, but it brought tears to Mr. Franklinson's eyes.

"Yes," he said. "I will miss her."

On her way out the door she experienced a sudden sense of having done the best she could for her aunt.

She'd warned her about Cap.

She'd brought her orchids.

She'd said good things about her to an old friend.

She was making sure she had a respectful burial.

As she drove to Aunt Billie's oceanfront cottage, she noticed a persistent rattle from the dashboard. Once the car was parked in the garage, she reached inside the glove compartment.

The Ladysmith was still in there along with the perfume atomizer. She slipped the items out of the glove compartment. She would store the gun away while she thought about what to do with it. She wasn't sure what to do with the perfume, but she carried both with her.

It was a relief, as she walked across the road, no longer having to avoid the two people who had sent her away. Cap was still missing. Police thought he had had been wounded and was probably dead somewhere in the wilderness. And Aunt Billie was not going to show up. Eden was free to live at the lodge again.

She had already emptied her backpack, setting her clothes in a drawer, and returning the papers from CJ's to the concealed compartment in Jess's closet. With the addition of the gun and perfume, the lid refused to fit.

Eden removed the contents. She had assumed the folded newspaper ad pages served as lining for what she knew from long ago to be the rough wood of the unfinished compartment bottom. But in removing the ad pages to enlarge and deepen the space, a thin piece of wood cut to the dimensions of the compartment came up with them, revealing two slim notebooks beneath.

The words "Aviator Flight Log" were lettered on their outside covers. She glanced through a few pages of one of the notebooks, confirming it contained entries for flights made by her grandfather. She'd study these later.

Without the newspaper advertising pages, everything fit. Eden replaced the lid and started across the room when she unfolded the pages to make sure there was nothing more than advertisements inside. A story beneath a series of advertisements caught her eye with its headline: "Police Seek Cold Case Help."

The page was dated from early in 2013, before Jess vanished. Jess had likely taken the paper from the table in the common room where newspapers and magazines were kept for guests. The story consisted of a few paragraphs. Eden hadn't gotten far when Ruth called to her from downstairs.

"Would you take some soap and fresh towels to Mr. Hayes's room? You can leave the things outside his door."

Eden said, "Beach, bath, face, or hand towels?"

Ruth said, "Give him one of each."

"Yes, ma'am."

She glanced at the article again. A paragraph had been starred with a faint pencil mark. Jess had seen the article and was interested enough to keep it in a place where it wouldn't get tossed out by accident. Eden read the paragraph.

The story was about a young woman named Lily Palmer who had gone missing after a fire at the Golden Cove seaside hotel and boardwalk in 1988. The young woman had no home in the area. Eden realized Jess's interest in the past and in the homeless might be the fundamental thing about her cousin she ought to pay more attention to.

Her thoughts turned to the matchbook with the initials GC Hotel printed on little golden waves. She had found the matchbook on the floor near a wall in the room Bobby Hayes occupied. It was possible another visitor had left it behind. Still, she would ask if he had stayed there. He might have met Lily Palmer. He might have spoken with Jess about the fire and Lily.

She was startled at the buzzing of her phone.

"You said if I came up with anything about your cousin to call you."

"Wanda?"

"I found a book with a few pages of writing in it. The name Jess was on the inside flap of the diary. It might've belonged to her."

"Where was it?"

"Thrift store. They put books in bins above the clothes. I was looking at clothes first and then books, and this one caught my eye. I'm always looking for blank paper and there was mostly blank paper inside. The cover was a nice blue and green. I looked, and I saw her name on the inside flap. If it's your cousin's diary, how come it's in a thrift store?"

"My aunt got rid of most of her things." Her books, the shell collection, and most of her clothes were gone, although her sandals and a red dress were still hanging in the closet. And the fox and mermaid posters remained on the wall of her room.

"Did you read any of it?"

"There weren't many pages with writing, but no, I didn't."

"I'll come get the diary."

"I don't have it. I didn't have the money for it."

"Where is the store?"

"Around the corner from Harbor Place. It closes in another hour."

Eden was about to knock at Mr. Hayes's door when she heard voices. It was probably from a radio or TV with the volume turned low. She left the soap and towels for him on a table next to his room and went out by the east porch.

**

At the thrift store, she crossed a gray concrete floor and paused where a woman was examining a handful of DVDs. The woman returned one of them to a box of books and DVDs above a clothing display for plus-size women's jeans. There was a remote chance, and Eden asked. "Have you come across a diary? With a colorful cover?"

A DVD fell from the woman's hand and clattered on the spotless concrete. "Can't you see I'm busy?" She looked everywhere but at Eden.

Eden picked up the fallen item and handed it to her. A wheeled cart next to the woman was loaded with DVDs, books, and clothes.

"You're buying all these things for yourself?"

"Going to hospitals. Nursing homes. I care about others. Unlike some people."

"Yes, people can be uncaring."

"Tell me about it."

The woman moved on toward the furniture and children's toys heaped against white walls trimmed with blue. Eden checked until she'd gone through every place where books were offered in the store.

Nothing resembling the diary Wanda described turned up. The number Wanda called from was recorded on Eden's phone. There was a brief delay and she heard a lot of background noise: hairdryers, music, laughter. Wanda's voice came to her.

"You found the diary *where*?"

"Women's plus-size jeans."

Eden rechecked the display. No diary. The cashier was already filling the woman shopper's bags. Eden hurried over to her.

"Ma'am, the diary I mentioned with the colorful cover? It may have been sold already to someone other than you, but could I or would you take a quick look through your bags? I sure would appreciate it."

"It must be important."

"I think it belonged to my cousin. She's missing."

The cashier gave Eden a sympathetic look and spoke to the woman across the top of her register. "The book she described is in one of your bags. I put it in there."

Before the woman could say anything, the cashier reached inside a bag and pulled out a book with a blue and green cover. She handed it to Eden.

"Here. Take a look."

Eden felt the floor move beneath her. She recognized Jess's large scrawl. And her name was on the inside flap. She turned to the shopper. "Could I buy this from you?"

The woman snatched it from Eden's hand and held Jess's diary out of reach. Her glance was sly.

"How much will you pay me for it?"

"Have a heart." The cashier's voice was disapproving.

The woman turned on the cashier. "She tells us a story about her cousin. This book might have a treasure map hidden in it. It could be the diary of a celebrity who's written bad things. It could make me rich."

The cashier checked the receipt. "Look through it. I bet you won't find anything of value like you're hoping for. Give this girl a break. You paid a quarter for it."

The woman thumbed through the diary, her mouth moving as she read. No treasure map fell out. After a moment she sighed. "It's too bad about your cousin, dear," she said. "You can have her diary for five dollars. Take it or leave it."

It was the last of Eden's cash.

Chapter Thirty-three

Jess had used stars to mark the entries in her diary while the names of some of the people she mentioned were indicated by initials. Eden knew who the people were. She settled halfway up the big dune with the ocean spread before her like a patchwork quilt, and she began to read:

When I mentioned my idea of writing about missing and homeless girls, CJ told me about a girl named Lily. She had worked a few days for us before she left and later disappeared after a fire at the hotel she worked at, the Golden Cove. The fire was the summer of 1988 or 1989, CJ said, which was before I was born. This was the first I'd heard about Lily or the fire.

Cap and Mom were laughing about getting hold of CJ's will and making it say what they wanted, like it was a big joke to them. Well, it has been hidden. They won't be laughing in the end.

E and I saw a fox. It was scrawny. I told her even though it had been a hard life for it here, this place by the sea was a home. CJ named the Fox Dunes Lodge for the animals. We'll make sure no one takes their home from them, E said. I told her if anything happened to me, I'd find a way to remind her to keep her word.

***Lily's last name is Palmer. CJ said a group from the lodge combed the hotel area and the fox dunes wilderness. They found one of her shoes in the dunes and a knife. The police believed she was murdered in the dunes but her body has not been found. CJ said he thought one or two of our current guests had stayed at the hotel and had been part of the search party. I'm going to ask around and get an interview.

The diary ended there. Eden pulled out her phone and selected a number. Ruth had many friends and jobs to take care of. She looked at the phone in disbelief when Ruth answered.

"Do you remember the name Lily Palmer?"

Without any hesitation, Ruth said, "She was a sweet young lady who worked a few days for us. Then she went to work at a hotel south of here, and she disappeared after the Golden Cove fire. I haven't heard anything more. Is there some news?"

"I came across her name, and I understand some of our guests came here when the hotel burned. Some of them may have gone on a search party from the lodge, too. Do you recall any of their names?"

Ruth thought it over. "Everyone I can think of from the lodge went on the search for her. The party consisted of your grandfather and me, also Cap, Billie, and Mr. Hayes. He came to us after the fire, along with Mr. and Mrs. Jenkins. I think I heard Mr. Jenkins and his wife are dead, but Lily was friendly with him and his wife and with Mr. and Mrs. Scott. They both had arthritis. Come to think of it, I don't recall the Scotts going on the search."

"I'll go knock on Mr. Hayes's door."

"He's gone visiting south of here. He'll be back in a few days." Eden hadn't noticed his beige compact car missing from the parking lot.

After she'd ended the call, she realized she had another question for Ruth. She wondered if any of the same people in the search party for Lily Palmer had also searched for Jess. Ruth was unavailable, so she left a voicemail.

Eden thought about Lily and Jess working at the lodge. On the other hand, many years separated them, and Lily's time at the lodge had been brief.

Eden closed the diary and zipped it into her backpack. She slipped her arms through its straps and walked down the dune until she reached a place where she could climb onto the walkway. She followed its wooden planks across the shallow valley of flowers toward the beach.

She thought about Cap and Aunt Billie, Scooter and his sister Kathy, Meg, and Johnny. All had motives to kill Jess. Aunt Billie and Cap to gain possession of the lodge if they thought or knew Jess was the heir. Cap may have feared being exposed as a fake veteran. Cap and Scooter might have decided Jess threatened the drug business Eden believed they operated. Scooter's sister Kathy knew Johnny loved Jess and wouldn't marry Kathy even though he was the father of her child. She suspected Meg less than the others, but if she thought Jess was going to leave her, Meg could easily have killed her on a dive and hidden her body. Johnny might have done it out of anger over losing her and the lodge. His evasions in talking about Jess and going into hiding after Aunt Billie's murder were deeply troubling. Eden may have blinded herself to the real possibility of his guilt.

Something doglike on swift legs trotted toward her across the shallow valley below the walkway. She watched it make its way between the tangled stems of flowers and clumps of tall sea oats. It stopped, lifted its head, and stared at her from yellow eyes. It held a silver fish in its mouth. For a moment she felt close to something wild and beautiful. The red fox was going home to feed its young.

Jess and Lily never had the chance.

The fox disappeared in the dunes undergrowth. Eden took the walkway steps to the beach. Raynell came running toward her from farther down the shore. She slowed as she drew near Eden, but she kept her eyes averted as she sashayed the last few steps to her side. She had something on her mind.

"Why don't you sit down?" Eden said. "And we'll talk."

"You promise not to scold me about coming here by myself?"

Eden made a quick decision. "I promise."

They sat on the beach. Waves like cat's paws kneaded and curled along the shore. Beyond the waves the body of the ocean rose and fell in the sun. Something made her turn. She glanced at the big dune behind them. She had the sensation they were being watched, but she saw no one.

"I'm going to visit with my daddy," Raynell was saying.

Her face was grave as she gave Eden this news. In the strong sunlight Eden noticed a reddish tint to Raynell's brown hair.

"Tell me about him."

Eden realized she hadn't given any thought to Raynell's family.

"I think I'll like him."

As if this fact had stirred something in her, Raynell jumped up and climbed the big dune. Eden glanced across her shoulder at the child. She could see her walking near some tangled vegetation before Raynell came back to her side. Raynell flopped down in the sand with a sigh, her arms hugged to her chest.

"You see something worrisome?"

"Not this time."

"You did before?"

"I'm not sure." She dug her toes in the sand, impatient with herself.

"I'd like to hear about it."

"This one time I saw a face. It was behind some leaves. I took a picture, but when I looked at it, the picture didn't show the face. I was too far away."

"I'll go look," Eden said. She found nothing human like a piece of trash or clothing in the bushes. She didn't find footprints. The sun beat down. She wished she had worn a hat.

She returned to Raynell and spread her empty hands wide. Raynell snapped her picture, and slipped her hand in Eden's, and they walked near the waves. The sunlight deepened the reddish tinge in Raynell's hair. And from the child's upturned face, Eden thought she saw Jess's eyes gazing into her own.

At the lodge, an envelope with her name on it had been left on the kitchen table. Eden opened it. She was relieved and strangely disappointed at what she found. She had grown used to receiving a message. This time the envelope was empty.

Chapter Thirty-four

The blades of the ceiling fan clicked with a broken sound. Eden sat across from Ruth at the kitchen table, watching the older woman pour glasses of iced tea from a pitcher beaded with moisture. Eden reached for a glass for herself, thinking back to Ruth showing her and Jess the proper way to serve guests in the dining room, Ruth letting them answer the phone and take reservations. With Ruth guiding them, the two young girls thought life was exciting and fine, and the world was theirs. Eden didn't think this any longer. Ruth took a long drink. The sun angled through tall pines beyond the screen door and window. Its sliding light moved along the walls and worn wooden floor before slipping away. Ruth set the glass aside. Her eyes found Eden's.

"Your grandfather and I didn't agree on things sometimes, but at least I have the satisfaction of having kept my promise to him on the matters I'm going to tell you, though I have been sorely tempted to break the promise." Ruth nodded as though trying to convince herself of the rightness of her decision.

She wondered what Ruth was leading up to. "Well, it's a fact CJ was impossible to get along with more than sometimes," Eden said, remembering his grumbling irritability. He never allowed her or Jess to hang around him for long. He preferred to be alone.

"This is how it was to be according to CJ's orders. You, as the youngest, were to reach twenty before what I'm about to tell you was to be revealed to you, Jess, or Luke. Jess and Luke are gone, but even so it wasn't my place to tell you before the appointed time. It's close enough to your birthday for me to go ahead and tell you this: your mother, Annie, was Jess and Luke's mother, too."

Eden felt as though she was swimming underwater at night during a storm. How was she to find her way in the dark tumult? Shock and disbelief rolled through her: Annie had given up the twins. They were her brother and sister.

Ruth said, "At the time when the twins were born, Annie was barely managing to take care of herself. And how your daddy's violent temper might affect your brother and sister made her crazy with worry. She asked CJ to bring them here. I taught them to read." She wiped sudden tears from her eyes with the back of her hand.

"The years went by, the twins were growing, Annie was doing much better, and she had you to take care of by then. Your daddy was dead, and there was all the moving around she did. It suited Annie to let the twins stay here."

"The babies weren't hers. How could Aunt Billie keep it secret?"

"This all happened around the time she moved back here from living in the West for a spell. She brought Cap with her. People assumed they were her babies, and she never said otherwise. The truth is they were decorations to her like those bright beads she used to wear."

Raynell walked into the kitchen. Eden was struck again by how much she resembled Jess. Her gaze shifted from Raynell to Ruth.

"She has Jess's eyes," she said.

Ruth nodded. "Yes," she said. "We'll talk more later."

Eden went upstairs and walked directly to the closet. She moved the cabinet to one side, knelt, and opened the hidden compartment. CJ's notebooks were on top, as if his ghostly hand had put them there so she would look at them first instead of the papers. They continued to frustrate her.

The notebooks and papers were all she had of him, and she wanted to be near him so he could steady her, like he had long ago when he had brought her to the lodge. It had been after Annie, in a stiff white jacket with her arms bound at her sides, was taken to a place where the doors locked with a heavy, sighing sound, not a jail exactly, but a place Annie couldn't leave for a while and Eden couldn't go in to see her when she wanted to.

Eden opened one of the notebooks. Several folded sheets slid out from between its pages. She set them aside and turned her attention to the details of places CJ had been and the airplanes he had flown. There had been a message taped to one of the covers. It said the books were intended for Jess, Luke, and Eden. CJ had left his notebooks to them so they'd appreciate he'd been a pilot once, a daring adventurer. He hadn't always been a grumbling angry old man.

She closed her eyes and pictured him flying the Corsair from the seabed floor at Red Parker's to a landing in Illinois. The Corsair saw duty way before CJ's time in Vietnam, but she knew he had always wanted to fly one. In her imagination, CJ landed the plane between a cornfield and pine forest near the Blue Moon sign.

She finished looking through the notebook and picked up one of the loose sheets. His mind was closing and his physical powers failing when he'd written it. This could explain why CJ's handwriting was like something driven. She was thinking about this when her phone buzzed.

"It's me, Wanda. I wanted to tell you I'm taking the bus to Chicago."

"You're going home."

"My brother says he can get me a job. He's working at a hotel, and I could be a housekeeper there. The pay and benefits are good."

Good pay and benefits. She was on a path to doing better for herself than Eden was. She hadn't made up her mind about school yet. Ted and his girlfriend were to marry as soon as the divorce went through. This was the one certainty in her life. She wished him happiness. Still, she didn't think the new wife would make spaghetti half as good as what she used to make.

"Pay and benefits. This is great news, Wanda."

"My boyfriend called from Miami. He wants me to meet him there, but I told him it was way too hot. Besides, I don't believe him when he says he's ready to settle. When I was with him before, every few months we'd be on the road. I can't take any more moving except for getting myself to Chicago. My nerves are shot. I am worn out."

"I moved around a lot with my mom. It's in my blood. I'd like to see the world."

"Did you find the diary at the thrift center?" Eden heard eagerness in her voice, and she wondered why she hadn't tried to reach Wanda to tell her.

"I did, Wanda, and it was Jess's. I'm sorry I didn't get hold of you earlier and thank you." What part of being a human did she need to work on more so she wouldn't treat someone like Wanda as though she didn't matter? She knew the answer. It was her heart.

"Well, you probably couldn't reach me anyway. I don't have a phone. You might want to check inside the back flap of the diary. I think there's a snapshot stuck in there."

"I'll take a look."

Eden didn't realize until she had ended the call but she hadn't told Wanda about Jess being her sister. Wanda would have liked to have heard this. Eden was still getting used to the idea.

Wanda was finding her way home. It was the place where people helped you and where you'd be called upon to help them one day.

But when there weren't others to be with, emotions were the family we each carried around inside ourselves. Encourage the good. Work with the hard ones. Then if anyone shows up knocking at the door, you'll be ready to bring them into your home. The family in your heart.

Eden tried to reach Wanda. Wherever she'd called from, nobody answered.

She removed Jess's diary from the compartment. Wanda was right. There was something stuck inside the back flap. Eden pried the old snapshot loose. Strips of the flap stuck to its face, but she could see enough between the stuck parts to tell she was looking at a picture of a young man.

He used to make her and Jess laugh as they solved math problems with his guidance. He'd bring a telescope with him to the dunes. Those were Cyril's interests. Math, the stars, and Jess.

It felt right, thinking of Cyril and Jess together. He would show her the stars in their places. She would tell him of the sea and its unruly ways. Their child, Raynell, would be with her daddy soon, staying in an apartment probably somewhere near where he taught. Eden wondered what it would be like going to a school as fine as MIT.

She returned her attention to CJ's notebooks. As she unfolded and examined the inserts from another of the books, she found herself reading some of the same scraps of sentences she'd read in the papers from CJ's cabin. But there was explanatory language. At last she understood what she hadn't been able to before.

What she was looking at were legal descriptions of the lodge and property CJ owned in the fox dunes along with properties in Jacksonville, Miami, and Orlando. There were orders detailing what was to become of it all: the lodge and property were to go to Jessica, Luke,

Ruth, Annie, and Eden. To Eden she was Jess, but Jessica had to be her sister's legal name. Everything had been witnessed, signed, and dated. It was CJ's will. Jess had hidden it here in his notebooks. CJ had never changed the will. He had never given up on Jess coming back to him.

Eden got up off the floor at the sound of the after-hours bell and walked downstairs.

Chapter Thirty-five

He said her name. She knew his voice, and she opened the door. He removed the black watch cap he wore low over his brow. In the glow from the porch light she saw the scar on his forehead from the fight he had with Luke about Jess. McCabe was a fighter like Luke, trained with guns, knives, his bare hands. He had probably been trained in deception.

"What brings you here, McCabe?" The lateness of the hour made her hesitate to let him in.

"Some things can't be said over dinner or the phone. I'm here to tell you more about Luke and me."

Eden stepped onto the porch and closed the door behind her.

"Okay," she said.

She listened while McCabe told her the village they'd entered had been thought to be friendly. It wasn't. Luke stayed behind to hold the enemy off while his wounded buddies were evacuated. She had read some of this in newspaper stories.

"He died in my arms as we were being airlifted out." This detail was new to her. She wondered if it was true. Luke had been so furious with McCabe they had been in a savage fight. The scar wormed across McCabe's forehead.

But it was also possible Luke had come to accept the likelihood of his twin's death. As he lay dying, it would be in Luke's nature to ask McCabe to find the killer.

McCabe confirmed her thinking with what he said next. "I promised Luke I'd come here to look for her and a murderer. But then you and I met and I sensed what the real reason was for you being here. You didn't want much, if any, help from me. You had to do this on your own."

He paused in the time it took for the song of the cicadas to rise and fall and rise again. "The fact is, I couldn't stay away. Not for long." McCabe's eyes searched hers.

Eden thought back to a night in the forest, Cap coming after her. "You scared Cap away the night he assaulted me. And then you kept an eye on me until you were certain I had reached the lodge."

"From what I saw, you were able to take care of yourself," McCabe said. "Except for one time."

She waited for him to explain. Instead, McCabe, who had been holding something at his side, took her hand in his and set in her palm a carved rectangular wooden box.

She had been unable to reach it the night of the fire at Cap's, the smoke overwhelming, the flames threatening. Someone had carried her from the inferno and taken her to CJ's.

McCabe's gaze was fixed on her own.

She told him Luke was her brother. McCabe nodded. She said she had been thinking of ways to attract the killer and trap him into revealing what he had done. Luke would approve, she said.

"You're going to lure a killer? If I could I'd order you not to try it. But orders wouldn't work with you." He asked her to promise to tell him before putting any plan into action.

Eden would make no promises.

After McCabe left, Eden walked upstairs to sit in her sister Jess's room. She gazed out the east window. In the moonlight, several foxes appeared on the spine of the dunes. Soon they were running over the dunes toward the sea.

She thought about how they hunt and breed in the whiteness of the moon, in the moist dark of evening. They lift their heads to the morning's gray light and to the rain. It soaks their fur and touches their skin. Sand clings to the fur between the soft pads of their paws. They live. They breed. And when they die, they leave behind their young to follow secret pathways through the dunes.

The pathways of sleep took Eden to the opening of a hidden den, and she crawled inside.

Heavy with dreams, she reached out to touch a muzzle, a patch of rough fur. She felt warm breath on her hand.

She was their captive. She was home.

Yellow eyes closed.

Chapter Thirty-six

Midway on the stairs between the second floor and the common room, Eden paused to listen. There was a slight sound coming from the direction of Ruth's apartment at the back of the lodge. It was possible Ruth and Raynell had returned from the birthday party they'd gone to across town. If they had, there would be talk and laughter, but this was not what she'd heard. It was a furtive sound. She glanced over the banister. A shadow moved on the hallway wall. When she saw the top of a straw safari hat, Eden was relieved to remember he had returned from a visit farther south.

"Hi, Mr. Hayes," she called.

He looked up. "Why, hello," he said. He removed the hat and gave her a wave.

She reached the ground floor as he rounded the corner of the hall and entered the common room, a brown leather bag in one hand. He wore a summer-weight suit and a white shirt open at the collar.

"Can I help you with anything, Mr. Hayes?"

291

"Yes," he said, glancing along the hallway in the direction he'd come from. "I couldn't locate Ruth, and I have something for her. Where is she?" He held up a sealed business envelope. "I have written her a check. It is for a small amount. I do wish it could be more," he said.

"They were expected home soon." She peered beyond the screen porch. "But as I'm sure you know, a big storm's coming. They'll stay in town, most likely," Eden said.

"They?"

"Raynell and Ruth."

"Yes, I see." With a slight frown, he handed her the envelope. "I would have preferred to thank her in person, but I'll be leaving soon," he said. He took a few steps in the direction of the porch. He faced her. "I will probably miss them. This is especially regrettable because, you see, I've decided to make it my last visit."

"I'm sorry to hear this from you, Mr. Hayes. You've been coming to the lodge for many years."

"I'll be going south in the future, although I may decide to go west next time. Possibly north. Since my wife died, I have time to travel. And there is much to see and do."

He bowed his head and brought his hand to his mouth, the light sound he made somewhere between a throat clearing and a cough. He removed his hand. "I am old, but I am renewed each day. I'll have to wait and see where life takes me." His smile was fleeting.

"Do you have a picture of your wife with you?"

"No, no I don't carry any," he said, quickly adding, "of course I have many at home, all nicely framed and hung on the walls."

"Mr. Hayes, I hope your decision to make this your last visit doesn't mean you have complaints about staying here?"

"No, everything has always been quite to my liking." The shy smile returned for an instant, then wavered and vanished.

"It is our loss. Do you have a minute? There's something I've been meaning to ask you."

"Yes, Eden?"

She couldn't explain why the sound of her name was suddenly jarring, as though a secret familiarity colored the way he spoke it, and this gave it an oddly intimate quality. And yet there had been something impersonal about it, too, as if the word had been shaped inside a breath of ether.

"Does the name Lily Palmer mean anything to you?"

He gave serious attention to an area rug. "No," he said, his gaze drifting to the stairs. "Is she someone I ought to meet?" He tilted his head, a flirtatious smile playing across his mouth. His eyes caught hers.

"She went missing after a fire at the boardwalk and Golden Cove Hotel. She'd worked there. Ruth said you were a guest. Were you there when the fire broke out?"

He hesitated before replying. "It was a lovely old place. After the fire I came here, as did several others. I kept a matchbook as a memento. I believe you recovered it while dusting in my room."

"Yes, I did. Can you tell me anything about the night of the fire?"

"Why do you care, Eden? It was well before you were born."

"I might write a story about it."

"History is the past. I am interested in the present," he said, his eyes bright with something like amusement as he looked at her, "and the future. Well, to answer your question, it was unfortunate. I lost all my luggage except for this one piece. I brought it with me to the lodge the night of the fire." He glanced at the bag. He had set it on the floor.

"Lily worked at the lodge a short time before she took a job at the hotel. Ruth said you went on the search party organized for her by our lodge. Are you sure you don't remember anything having to do with Lily Palmer?"

Mr. Hayes cocked his head with a thoughtful expression. "As a result of the additional information you have given me, I do recall going out with others to look for a young woman. We came across a shoe believed to belong to the young woman you spoke of. It was, I believe, in the dunes, but my memory is no longer fresh the way it once was." He stared intently at her. "It was terrible, finding those things."

"There was something else beside the shoe?"

"A knife was found there, isn't this so?" He smiled.

"Your memory is better than you think, Mr. Hayes. By the way, you of course remember Jess? Jess was writing a paper about Lily. She was going to ask someone from here for an interview about the fire and the search. I wondered if she'd asked to speak with you and if you'd talked with her?"

Mr. Hayes studied the wall on the far side of the room. "You are the first person to bring up the subject with me. Perhaps she spoke with another guest?"

"It's possible."

He glanced at his wristwatch several times. She reminded herself nervousness didn't indicate guilt. If it did, she would have been jailed long ago. He was anxious about his taxi and his flight what with the coming storm. Its low rumblings were closer.

"Ruth will understand you had to catch a plane and couldn't wait for her," Eden said, trying to put him at ease. "And don't worry. I'll make sure she gets your gift." There was something else she wanted to ask.

"Before you go, Mr. Hayes. You were here the summer Jess disappeared. Were you in the search party for her? You knew her. What do you think happened to her?"

Wind gusted at the southeast area of the common room and the large fireplace there. Mr. Hayes gazed past Eden's shoulder toward the sound. Looking at him she realized his hair was the color of ashes.

"May I ask the reason for all the questions? Do you think I had something to do with the disappearances of the unfortunate young women? Whatever happened to them occurred long ago.

"If you will excuse me, I must go and wait for my taxi or I might miss it and be left behind."

She had offended him, and she hadn't learned anything. Except Mr. Hayes was defensive and unfeeling.

He picked up his bag and walked out onto the porch, blending with the shadows as he stared through its screen into the dark.

Chapter Thirty-seven

Eden walked upstairs to the bathroom at the landing, closing the door behind her. A quick twist of the faucet sent a stream of water gushing into the big claw-footed tub. Her clothes fell to the floor. As she soaked in the hot water, she heard a vehicle door slamming. Mr. Hayes was on his way to the airport. Eden pulled on Jess's red dress with its pockets and inspected herself in the bathroom's full-length mirror.

The wind was rising. She hurried along the drive, the dress pressing against her curves, the rhinestones on Jess's sandals sparkling. She crossed the road to a footpath leading between the dunes. Waves roared along the shore.

Eden took off the sandals, carrying them with her as she moved north along the edge of the waves. When she reached the wooden walkway, she slipped her backpack from her shoulders and left it with the sandals on wooden planks still warm from the sun. She jumped from the walkway into the sand at the side of the big dune and climbed midway, where she settled.

Overhead, a lone helicopter moved through the clouds, its navigation lights flashing. On the far horizon, a ship plowed the waters above Red Parker's. The reef was shrouded in darkness from the coming storm.

Earlier in the heat of the long afternoon she had been here and had called his name. A brushing sound and the rustling of leaves along with a stirring in her blood were enough for her to believe he had seen her. He would look for her to show up here again.

The sound of footsteps along the walkway sent a shiver through her. She wanted to cry out at the sight of his shuffling gait and the way his hands hung as though lifeless at his sides.

He was coming toward her from the beach. Eden plunged along the side of the dune to meet him, Johnny reaching for her hand and helping her step onto the planks.

She circled her arms around him, holding onto him as though he was the one who was drowning this time, and she was saving him. He was as thin as he once had been when she was a child and he was a half-starved boy. They stood apart looking at each other, distant lightning falling across the sky. They climbed high onto the slope and sat facing the sea.

There was a fixed brightness in his gaze. "Eddie, this won't be easy," he said.

"Like anything is."

He pulled a gun from under his shirt.

"Still, I didn't think you would shoot me," Eden said.

"It's for you." He held it out to her. "I want you to take it."

"Why?"

"You're mostly by yourself at the lodge."

Aunt Billie's Ladysmith was in the secret compartment in her room. "I already have a weapon," she said. "You can keep this one."

He slipped the revolver in a carrier belt under his shirt. "When you hear what I'm about to say you may never want to see me again. But this is a chance I will have to take if we're ever going to be together. And I want to be with you, Eddie. More than anything."

He took a deep breath, his hands dangling across his knees. He stared at the sea. "Jess had sunk into one of her moods. She asked me to take her out to the reef. She loved it there. But it's dangerous. And it was late."

Eden said, "Could she have been depressed because she wanted you and thought you had taken up with me?" With a heavy heart she was thinking of her and Johnny three years ago. Depending on how he answered, she might never be able to live with herself again.

Johnny picked up a handful of sand and let it sift through his fingers. He said, "She didn't want me. She wanted to go night diving. We had done it before to prove we could. This time I wound up telling her the reef was too far and it was too late. We argued a lot toward the end. Then I got her to at least listen to the idea of us going in right here from the beach and exploring around the old pier. Before I tell you the rest of what happened with Jess, there's something else."

He hesitated, gazing at Eden with the fixed bright stare she had seen earlier. It made her uncomfortable.

"Go on."

He held out his hands, inspecting them front and back as if a stranger's hands had slipped like gloves over his own. He ran his hands through his hair and looked down. She could not see his eyes.

"His face was red and swollen from booze. His knuckles were bloodied from hitting me. He'd get drunk and cause fights over the stupidest things. Even an effing can of Bondo one time. Sent the other guy to the hospital with parts of his face hanging loose.

"I was sick of him. We'd been fishing at a jetty. When he came at me, I punched him. He fell and his head cracked on the rocks. Eddie, I killed my father.

"Scooter and I were buddies at juvie. We looked out for each other." His voice suddenly hard, his face drawn with lines of suffering. "I swore I'd never spend even one hour in a prison. Then I found a home at the lodge with Luke and Jess.

"The night she disappeared, I left Jess here while I went to get us dive equipment at the marina. I made time pass slowly. She'd agreed to go in at the pier, but I figured delaying getting back to her would be like insurance, there'd be no more argument about the reef.

"When I got here, I couldn't find her. I looked around and there was a small campfire, the coals still burning. This made me think she had met someone and wandered down the beach with them. She'd come back eventually. It had happened before."

The wind made a crying sound in the trees.

"Where was she, Johnny? Where did you find her?"

He pointed in the direction of undergrowth and sea oats at the base of the dune. "She was on her stomach facing the waves, like she'd tried to run into the water to get away. I turned her over. She'd been carved up so bad." Johnny covered his face with his hands. Eden sat beside him, unable to speak.

When she heard his voice again, it was filled with anguish and fury. "Whoever killed her must've heard me coming. They ran but they left the knife behind. I'm standing over her with the knife when Miss Billie shows up, and she's all, 'You did it, Johnny, you killed her.' She's hysterical, and I'm like, 'No way,' and I'm crying and trying to tell her what had happened.

"She relented, saying she'd been out looking for Jess, finally remembering to come for her here. I mean it was her favorite place, on land anyway. Miss Billie said she'd hoped to have a serious talk with her, which was total bull----. She wanted to find Jess to be sure Jess would go to work in the morning. They'd had a fight earlier.

"Miss Billie knew about my past, and she said because of what I did to my father, and because she'd have to testify as to finding me standing over the body with the bloody knife in my hand, there wasn't a soul who would believe I hadn't killed Jess. And there was the fact of Jess breaking up with me. Billie said she'd tell the jury good things about me, but she figured for sure I'd go to prison."

"You believed what she said?"

"She'd let me make the lodge my home and supported me working there, Eddie, and it was easier to see things her way and go along rather than argue. I couldn't risk losing the brother I found in Luke, steady work, three meals a day, and a real bed to sleep in.

"Cap showed up at the dune about the same time as Billie, and I guess I'd already gone crazy because, exhibit one, when Billie found me I was gripping the knife and exhibit two, I let Cap and your aunt persuade me to do some things I've been paying for ever since."

Johnny gazed out to sea.

"What were those things?"

"Cap made clear how if I were to think over my circumstances, I'd conclude it would be in my best interest to help out Scooter and him in their business. He made it sound easy, like I'd make good money. He was right about the money."

Eden asked, "What would it be, the business?" It had to be someone else sitting beside him asking this question. Because she knew what the answer was already, and because she felt as though she was somewhere else.

Johnny said, "You might have seen it on TV a while back, a van overturned on the interstate up in Georgia? Bags of dope busted out from the smashed bellies of frozen fish, coolers and fish all over I-95. I worried the load might be traced to Cap and Scooter and me even though they have been real careful. I mean, it's not like we had designer labels on anything. The driver never said a word. He died in the accident. And nobody traced the truck back to a visit at the lodge."

"What kind of drugs?" The trees were tossing in the strengthening wind. Her voice came from somewhere high in the branches.

He counted them off on his fingers. "Crack, weed, meth, hash, fentanyl, heroin, coke, anything a customer wanted to inject, swallow, or snort, we got it for them. I'm not proud of any of it. Scooter had his big boat for transporting stuff up from Miami. He used the boat for a meth lab, but after a fire he figured it wasn't a good idea. Which brings me to the next thing I agreed to."

Eden braced herself.

"I buried Jess."

A deep cold wrapped itself around her.

"Where?"

"Scooter and I took her out to the reef."

She wasn't sure she heard him right.

"The reef?"

Johnny wiped his arm across his brow. He said, "We went out to the old airplane wreck. She loved that place." He gazed toward Red Parker's. "Hardly anyone ever goes there, probably never at night. I left the knife somewhere out there, too."

Her thoughts spun crazily to the small glittering thing she'd seen at the Corsair, wondering if it could have been part of the necklace she'd given Jess on her last visit to the lodge. If she'd worn it this would be a sign Jess had loved her still.

She heard a stranger's voice asking him, "Did she have on a necklace?" She had to have an answer.

Johnny shook his head. "I can't say. The condition of the body—" He left the sentence unfinished. And she recognized she was crazy for asking.

"You knew what had happened to her all along." Eden's voice was clotted with rage. "What you did meant her killer might never be found. You're a liar, Johnny. Every day you were with me was a day of lies."

She drew back, and then she was pummeling his shoulder with her fists. He took her blows, head bowed to his chest, his hands clenched on his knees, and the thing she'd been trying to push away all summer came slamming into her.

"Why should I believe you weren't the one to have killed her? I think you did, Johnny. You killed Jess. Say it."

"No," he said, his voice gentle. "I wasn't the one."

Johnny reached for her, Eden pulled away, but it felt as if she could barely move, like she was trapped underwater, her air had been cut off, and she would never breathe again.

"Listen to me, Eddie. This summer when you showed up, I thought I had a chance with you," he said. "See, I never forgot us together. And you came back, and it's been good with us. Well, mostly. I didn't want to mess things up. So I'm telling you the truth. And asking you, in time, to understand and forgive."

She was silent, struggling to absorb what had happened to Jess. Pain took her back in time to the woods near the Blue Moon.

A light snow had begun to fall when she came upon the fox in a clearing. Wind touched its fur. Soon the fox would be buried in snow. Its eyes were open with death.

The day Eden told Jess about her and Johnny, she had thought Jess would say, "Johnny's yours, Eden. We've broken up for the last time." Jess hadn't said anything. Instead, she had stared at Eden from unblinking eyes.

Eden looked out to sea, and finally she knew how Jess had gotten caught in her mind with the fox in the snow. When she had gazed into her eyes, Eden had seen some part of Jess dying.

Jess had turned from her. She had walked into the shadows of the lodge. Eden hadn't been able to find her before leaving for Chicago later in the day. Jess hadn't returned her phone calls, texts, or letters. Several weeks later, she had disappeared.

Eden jumped up and started toward the waves. She wanted to wash herself clean and go back to the time before she had been with Johnny, when Jess had still loved her. She wanted to go back to a time before she had betrayed her sister. A time when Jess was still alive.

She told him she had learned Jess was her sister.

Johnny reached for her hand.

"Damn you, Johnny," Eden cried, pulling free of him.

"I'm already damned," Johnny said, his voice growing faint beneath the rising wind.

"You say you want me. Don't you ever think of anything but what *you* want? What about your daughter?"

"Angela," he said. He faced into the wind. The waves swallowed the beach. The moon and sun seemed to have come up and gone down several times before Johnny straightened his shoulders and gestured toward the wilderness.

"Going to collect my things. Then I'll be heading to the police station. One day you'll forgive me. There's a place for us, Eddie. No matter what, I'll always love you." He turned from her, his shirt filling with wind as if the boy he once had been was sailing away.

From out on the road a droning engine slowed as a pickup entered the clearing, pebbles and shells bouncing off its undercarriage. Eden hurried to retrieve her backpack and sandals at the end of the walkway.

From there she jumped to the beach and ducked under the planks. Footsteps above indicated two people were up there. She had invited one of them to meet her at the dunes for a drink and to dance, like old times.

She believed he was Jess's killer.

"Hey, Johnny, have you by any chance seen Eden? She told me to meet her here, and I figured it would be a real good time, her and me, a few drinks and a joint, some dancing. And the excitement of the storm. Instead, I run into you, old buddy. I guess you got to her before I did. Got her ready for me, huh?"

"She's gone, Scooter."

He tipped the cowboy hat, Scooter grinning. "Did she work on you to tell the police about our little business? So you and her could start a new life after you'd served reduced time for hiding Jess's body and dealing drugs?"

"Listen, Scooter, it was over between her and me before it even got started."

"Hey, I'm sorry, dude." He shook his head. "I don't suppose you listen to the news, being way out here?"

"No phone or internet, Scooter. No radio or TV. No newspaper delivery, either. But I look on the bright side. The situation helps me keep expenses under control. And I feel sure you're going to fill me in."

"They found Cap."

"Where?"

"'Gator Lake at the lodge. Some of his remains were on the little island." Scooter said, "You remember the developer who was shot and dumped in a car trunk? His partner, Mitch something, was about to board a plane when the police arrested him. He had some of Cap's guns with him and forged papers giving him ownership of the lodge. They charged the guy with his partner's murder. I'm speculating here but it could be the guy they nailed at the airport might have done both Cap and Billie."

"They'll want to question me."

"You haven't answered me, Johnny. You need to swear you wouldn't turn yourself in and talk to the police. You start talking, they'll send you to prison. I'm the one friend you have left and the closest thing you've got to a family. I've been like a dad to you. We should look out for each other the way Cap used to."

"Yeah. Cap sure did have our best interests at heart."

"I'm glad you see the sense in what I'm saying. I need you to stay in the business, Johnny, because I trust you. I'm in charge with Cap out of the picture. Ever been to Columbia? Grab your bedroll. Let's get out of the rain. It's a pretty place, Columbia. And there's something else."

"You're going to tell me whatever is on your mind, Scooter. Something tells me you won't hold back."

"After we talk business, let's go on over to the lodge. I feel sure we'll find Miss Eden there. The three of us can have some fun together."

She didn't hear Johnny's response, if there was one. Their footsteps faded. Her phone buzzed at the bottom of her backpack. She dug for it. She didn't recognize the number but thought it best to answer. The only sound was of gusting wind.

The wind picked up grains of sand, flinging them against Eden's face, legs, and arms, stinging her lips. Lightning cut across the towering clouds. She shoved the phone into her backpack.

Eden ran south into the storm.

Chapter Thirty-eight

Lightning illuminated the windows of the lodge. Behind veils of rain, live oak limbs and branches thick with trailing moss fell to the driveway. Eden pushed open the east porch screen door. Rain, wind, and wet leaves followed her inside. At the entry to the common room she checked her phone for voicemail from the earlier call. There were no messages.

Using her phone flashlight, she navigated to a chest where lanterns were stored at the foot of the staircase. A flicker of lightning sent her attention to the second-floor landing. The beam from her phone flashlight illuminated a tall wardrobe next to the bathroom.

This wouldn't be the first time the bulky antique had been mistaken in the darkness for a person. She walked to the top of the stairs. Guestrooms were arranged around the balcony overlooking the common room below. She directed the light at the closed doors. They rattled in the wind. It was unnerving.

Eden returned to the chest at the foot of the stairs. Inside she found several lanterns wrapped in newspapers. There were no batteries installed. She passed through the dining area to the kitchen. At the sink she knelt and probed with the light beam inside a cabinet, turning up candles, matches, a sturdy flashlight, and batteries.

Once she'd set up the lanterns and candles, shadow shapes danced on the common room walls. Logs and small pieces of wood for kindling had been stacked beside the fireplace at the room's southeast wall. She dusted off the spider webs from the kindling, built a fire, and sat on the floor before it. Her face grew warm. Her clothes began to dry.

A current of air ruffled her hair. She stared behind her, feeling as though the lodge was a ruin inhabited by ghosts. She listened to the pounding rain and the wind's cry in the eaves. She could hear the wild roar of the surf crashing on the beach. Rolls of thunder shook the earth. Lightning sprayed across the sky as though flung from the cup of an angry god. Or goddess.

She sat before the fire thinking about Johnny's confession. Jess had been killed in the dunes if Johnny could be believed. He had found, and left behind in the ocean, a knife from the scene. A knife had also been found in the dunes during the search for Lily Palmer.

And fire. There had been fire at the hotel and fire on the beach. But the deaths were separated by more than two decades.

Her heart pounded at the sound of her phone.

There was no name listed with the number. But it was the same number from the call she'd taken earlier at the old pier. There had been no answer at the other end. It was humbling to find herself so hungry for human contact she went ahead and answered what she suspected was a spam call.

"Hello?"

"Hello." A faint cough filtered through to her.

"Mr. Hayes?"

"I was unable to contact you or Ruth earlier, thus I am relieved to reach you. There's been an emergency, and I must return. I hope it will not be an inconvenience."

"Why, what's up?"

The connection broke apart, but she heard the words "I" and "lost." Eden got up off the floor and went out to the porch where the connection would be better, if it lasted.

"Mr. Hayes, are you still there? What were you saying? I missed most of it. You'll need to repeat yourself."

"I left it behind. I do hope my return won't disturb you or plans you may have made for the evening? I see it's getting on toward midnight."

"What did you leave behind?" She waited for his response. Beyond the porch screen, a stab of lightning illuminated a pickup. It was parked across the road from the posts at the end of the drive.

"My wallet, Eden. It contains credit cards, my ID, and a small amount of cash along with some important names and numbers. Would you mind visiting my room to look for it? I will stay with you on the phone while you go and see if it is there."

"There's no electricity here. And the roads are flooded. You are better off staying where you are. I can always have it delivered to you once the storm lets up."

"There's no going back. The loss has made me quite agitated, Eden. Please hurry. I can't wait much longer for an answer."

"I understand," Eden said. She carried a lantern and a flashlight she'd taken from the kitchen as she walked into the guestroom where he had spent many summers. She placed the lantern on a table and held the phone to her ear as she looked with the help of the flashlight around and under the bed and the table.

"Eden, if I may ask, where are you?" The connection was holding.

"Your room, Mr. Hayes."

"It's quite possible the wallet slipped between the mattress and headboard. Would you look?" It

314

was probably fear of losing his valuable credit and identity cards making him so talkative.

"I'll look again." Eden did as she was asked. "Nothing to report. I'm going to the closet."

"Oh, excellent," he said. Approving. Then anxious. "What about the dresser?"

"Hang on." She detoured from her plan to go to the closet and went instead to the dresser. A search of all its drawers came up empty. But in the flashlight's beam she saw a matchbook with golden waves and the lettering GC Hotel. It was on top of the dresser.

The initials LP were scrawled inside its cover. She didn't recall any writing on the matchbook when she'd first seen it. She slipped it into her pocket to give to him. She noticed an ashtray filled with discarded cigarettes. She would clean the room thoroughly in the morning.

"Nope, still no wallet," Eden said. She took up the lantern but decided to set it nearby on the floor and use the flashlight as she made her closet check. Several blankets were stacked on a shelf inside. There were a few wire hangers.

"You haven't neglected the bathroom, have you?"

"I'm stepping over to it," she said.

"Wonderful."

The sight of the shower reminded her for an uncomfortable moment of the movie *Psycho*. She flung the curtain back, noticing the stain in the tub she had worked on. It refused to go away.

"Have you left my room, Eden? Did you return the shower curtain to its proper place?"

"I did. What about the kitchen or the dining room? Could you have left your wallet there?"

He sighed. Disappointed but patient. "I did not enter either of those rooms today. However, there is another possibility. I will continue to stay on the line and keep you company while you conduct your search. I do not want to leave you alone on a night such as this."

She had been acquainted with him for years, but the entire interaction was setting off alarm bells. "Where to, then?"

"Upstairs."

What possible reason would he have had to go there? And when? She felt the room tilt beneath her. She steadied herself by leaning against the wall. When he spoke again it was as if he had read her thoughts and wanted to reassure her.

"Of course, you might wonder why I found it necessary to be upstairs. You had stepped out for your daily run, and I heard something, and I thought someone was trying to get in through a window to your room, the one you shared with Jess? I am not sure why I would have left my wallet there, if in fact I did. A blankness sometimes comes over me when I am feeling stress. It may be the cause for such a lapse in attention."

"Did you ever find the source of the sound?" Her hands were sweating.

"I suspect it was a shutter in the wind, but I was not able to fully determine what it was. I can offer no explanations, Eden."

Sudden memories of Mr. Hayes came to her the way things will surface in the rain after being buried in the sandy soil. He went to lodge events, pleasant and cheerful and modest, dancing with Aunt Billie, watching from the shadows as Jess and Eden performed when Aunt Billie ordered them to show off dance routines at parties when they were little girls, young girls, teens.

And there was Jess's diary entry about Lily Palmer working at the lodge and the Golden Cove. Mr. Hayes had stayed at the hotel and the lodge where Lily and Jess had worked. This might amount to no more than coincidence. But Eden was convinced it was meaningful.

A frightening realization had taken shape. "After we talked in the common room, did you go to the airport as you had planned?"

His laughter sounded like a sob. "I stayed behind longer than I had anticipated. After talking with you I had a feeling Ruth and the little girl would return soon after all. I sent the taxi away, and I removed my bag from the porch to my room.

Perhaps you saw the matchbook with the initials on it?"

"I did, Mr. Hayes."

"I wrote out Lily Palmer's initials so I would not forget her if we spoke again."

"You anticipated we would?"

"I did. And so, you see, we are enjoying the opportunity."

"You should have told me of your decision to stay longer, Mr. Hayes. I had no idea you were still in the lodge when I went out." She was certain he had never left.

"Don't scold me, Eden. If you had turned and looked toward my room you would have seen me standing there, but, as you seem to be most of the time, you were in a hurry and I did not want to disturb you on your way to a date. You looked so pretty, Eden. You always do. Are you upstairs?"

"I am not there yet."

You looked so pretty. He had watched her in secret. Who else had done this same thing? The one who had written her notes had kept himself hidden. The voice in the notes and Mr. Hayes's voice were the same, gently threatening, intimate, and yet impersonal.

This was a game. It would last until he grew tired of it or the pressure to end it overwhelmed him. She was taking an awful risk, but she was counting on his continuing to enjoy the game. She had work to do.

"Mr. Hayes, my flashlight's not working properly. I did have a lantern, but I left it in your room." At the top of the stairs, she slid the switch several times between on and off, convinced he would see proof the flashlight was malfunctioning.

"Please do not worry, Eden. I will be here."

She walked into her room, pushing the door nearly closed behind her. In the glare of lightning, she saw the wallet in the middle of the bed on top of the sheets. Eden, still speaking to him on her phone, said, "I think I can find another flashlight. It will take me a few moments, and I need to set the phone down."

"Yes, dear."

She slipped the phone under the pillow. She stepped to the east window and raised it partway. Rain blew in. After raising the window, Eden made her way in the dark to the closet.

She closed its door, turned on the flashlight, and carefully lifted the little cabinet in the corner, setting it to one side, then removed the hidden compartment's lid. She leaned down and grasped the Ladysmith revolver she had taken from her aunt's car. It was something she should have done long ago, checking to see if it was loaded.

It was not. Still, Mr. Hayes wouldn't be aware of this. She considered the perfume atomizer. The idea of disabling Mr. Hayes by blinding him with the perfume appealed to her. But too much could go wrong.

On the other hand, if she wore perfume, Mr. Hayes would be lulled into thinking she was receptive to his advances, and then she might be able to get the answers she had to have about Jess and Lily.

She applied a small amount of perfume. It was more atrocious than she had thought. She returned it to the compartment, replaced the lid, and, taking the gun with her, switched off the flashlight.

She was about ready to play the game of making herself seem available so she could get from him what she wanted. She had planned on doing this with Scooter. But a person had to be flexible.

She walked again to the east window, where an updraft of cool air brought home the reality of climbing from the window, dropping to the porch roof below and to the ground. Luke, Johnny, Jess, and Eden all knew Aunt Billy would have been deep in the coffee brandy and wouldn't have noticed even if they'd marched down the main stairway shouting and singing on the way out. But it was more fun to hang off the windowsill and help each other down. Soon they would be on their way to the dunes.

The pickup was still parked across from the stone posts. If she could reach it, she'd be able to get help. Or would she? One thing was certain. After she had gotten the information she wanted from Bobby Hayes, she would need to reach the ground and run swift as a fox into the tangled vines and bushes.

She removed the phone from beneath the pillow. "Are you still there? You are patient, Mr. Hayes."

"I sometimes take years before one of my projects is ready."

She forced her voice to sound perky. "I've got the flashlight working." She made it flash, then turned if off. "Nope. It's gone out again. And I can't seem to find a replacement."

"Eden, my darling, I am close by your door." There was his small cough from the other end of the line.

The shadow had a cold. Raynell had said this while showing Eden a picture of a shape next to undergrowth at the big dune. A translation of what this meant came to her. The shadow had a *cough.* Had he been stalking Raynell?

"One minute, Mr. Hayes. I want to comb my hair."

Her heart banged in her chest at the sound of hurrying footsteps. One thing remained for her to do. She would get his confession while the police were on the way, and then she would escape through the window.

She pressed 9-1-1 on her phone.

"Eden?" he said. "What are you doing in there, dearest?" His voice, with a hurt tone in it, was coming from the hallway outside the bedroom door.

Her phone had gone dead.

She leaned against the windowsill, the gun in her right hand hidden behind her, the flashlight in her other hand. She had two weapons, and she faced the doorway.

He stood at the threshold, naked from the waist up, his skin glowing in the light from the lantern he held. The flesh hung in waxen folds on his narrow chest and from the muscles of his long arms. They were roped with veins.

His feet were bare. The belt from his pants was unbuckled, the loose buckle making a small ringing sound when he moved. The dress pants were snug across his waist. He'd eaten well this summer. He held his right hand behind him.

"There's good news, Mr. Hayes. Even with all my troubles, I found the wallet." She forced herself to project calm.

He gazed from Eden to the bed. "Such beautiful little girls." He stared at Eden. His eyes reflected the lantern light.

"Are you wearing perfume, Eden?"

"I am, Mr. Hayes."

"For me? It is quite alluring."

"I am glad you like it."

"Yes, I do. I liked Jess, too." His words were light and sorrowing. From this she was betting he wanted to talk about himself and his victims. In his notes he had expressed the desire for her to see him. He wanted to be seen, and he wanted to be heard.

His voice grew cold. "Little girls grow up so quickly and become difficult to manage. It's a pity."

"Was Lily Palmer a *difficult* young woman, Mr. Hayes?"

He stared at her a moment, thinking about the question. "It was the noise she made crying and begging."

"I hear you, Mr. Hayes. And was Jess *difficult*?"

"I wanted to touch Jess's face and hair, but she kept asking about the Palmer girl. I tried to kiss her. She would not let me. Yes, she was difficult. And so I did her a favor, like I did for Miss Palmer. Being difficult as they were would have made their lives a constant torment for themselves and others. I put them out of their misery. There are others."

He stepped toward her. "The window is open. Why is the window open, Eden? The rain is

323

coming in. Are you planning to abandon me?" It was a child's voice.

"Never mind." He hiked his shoulders to show he no longer cared. "I have a better idea." He held the lantern away from his body, gesturing with it as if to usher her to the bed.

"Come here," he said. He had concealed a butcher knife behind him. Eden saw its shadow.

Chapter Thirty-nine

When she did not go to him as he had commanded, he stepped closer, thrusting his face at her. She sprang from the windowsill, slamming the Ladysmith's handle against his mouth. He staggered, the knife and lantern falling from his grip. She came at him again, wielding the gun in one hand and the flashlight in the other. Bobby Hayes caught an upraised arm, twisted it behind her, and forced her to the floor, disarming her. He straddled her while pulling his belt through the loops, and he strapped the belt like a collar around Eden's neck. He wiped his arm across his injured mouth.

"You have let me down," he said. He climbed off her, and he picked up his lantern and knife, using the knife to prod her to her feet. He pushed her toward the door.

Eden stumbled. When she lifted her gaze, she saw the eyes of the fox looking at her from its poster on the wall. It gave her courage, thinking how the little animals fought when they were hunted, they fought to live, and so would she.

Fleeting images came to her of Jess and Luke, Ruth and CJ, and Raynell's smile. The room stopped spinning.

"Are you going to kill me like you did Lily and Jess?" She was startled to hear the determined steadiness of her voice.

He shoved her outside the room to the top of the stairs. He jerked the leash. "We shall see, depending on whether your attitude toward me improves."

He shook the leash again, playful despite the injured mouth. She had not hit him hard enough.

"Where are you taking me?"

"You've been there often."

He grabbed the shirt he'd discarded on a chair in the common room. He tossed it across his shoulder, slipped on the shoes he'd left by the chair, and he marched her through the south porch out to the rain-soaked path.

A few stars were beginning to show. The yellow eye of the moon watched from between swift clouds. They walked to the toolshed and the Chevy parked outside its door. Bobby Hayes kicked her into the shed.

The smell of oily rags, paint, gasoline, and lethal chemicals dropped over her like a hood. He flipped a switch. Light from a single bulb illuminated a length of clothesline looped on a peg by the door. He removed it and bound her hands behind her.

When he was done, he leaned down and grasped an orange plastic container. She wanted to think he intended to gas up the Chevy, but when he marched her to the car, he set the container in front on the passenger seat. He might have another use for it in mind. She didn't want to dwell on the possibilities.

From the backseat she watched him pull on his shirt and button it, as though he was savoring the evil he had done and was going to do. He stepped into the car and turned the key in the ignition.

Floodwater threatened to swamp the Chevy as the old car turned onto the main road. The pickup was still parked across from the stone posts.

Eden tried to see inside the vehicle. She wasn't sure if she saw behind its window a shape hunched at the steering wheel. She did not recognize the pickup as belonging to anybody she knew. It bore a temporary tag.

They were heading north when she began work freeing herself. The loudness of the Chevy muffler disguised any sound her movements might have made. She was grateful for the cheap clothesline he'd used to bind her. Eden's hands were tied. But her thumbs were free. If they had not been, her hands would have been like paws.

She felt the cheap rope easing as she worked on it. The car lurched into and out of flooded potholes, the gas container finally tipping over with a sloshing sound and a soft thump. Bobby Hayes reached for it with a casual familiarity. He was used to being around the flammable liquid.

Fumes filled the car. The cheap perfume she wore was no match for the gasoline odor. He cranked the window down and continued to guide the car to the big dune. He parked at the walkway and switched off the ignition.

"What happened to the car you had earlier?"

"Questioning me won't buy you time, Eden."

"I asked because I am interested in you, Mr. Hayes."

"In me?" The voice was childlike in its sudden undisguised need.

"Yes," she said.

He gazed through the windshield at the ocean. It wasn't long before he began talking. He wanted to make sure she heard all about him before he took her life.

"Let me start with Miss Lily Palmer. She waited on my table at the Golden Cove, a sweet little thing, and we talked as she brought food and drink to me. She was underage, and she had run away. She was desperate to establish a bond.

"I saw how lovely Miss Palmer was, and I believed I could help her. I took her dancing at the boardwalk pavilion. I bought her cotton candy and toys. I bought her drinks. The finest wine."

He continued to stare at the horizon where a brilliantly lighted ship plowed the waves. For the briefest of moments, Eden allowed herself to believe someone would rescue her. But she knew thinking this was a futile waste of energy, so she began planning what she might do to save herself once she had the full use of her hands.

The rope no longer bound her as tightly as it once had. Even so, she knew her options were limited. If she could time it exactly, she could slam the car door into him when he opened it to get at her. If she could do this, throwing him off balance, Eden was confident she could escape.

She was fast, she knew the dunes, and she could swim. But still she was far from certain she could push the door into him at the right moment and with enough strength to disable him. If something went wrong, she might not get another chance to escape.

Mr. Hayes was saying, "Miss Palmer and I enjoyed the boardwalk for quite some time. However, it was noisy with laughter and shrieks from the rides, and it got on my nerves. I can still hear the noises."

She could try bailing out. But she needed to get more information about Jess and Lily. Johnny had said Jess was buried at Red Parker's Reef. She wondered what Mr. Hayes might tell her. And she had to find out where Lily was buried. She must get Mr. Hayes to talk about both young women.

And the more she thought of attempting to escape, the memory of how difficult it was to open the old car doors came to her. She would have to come up with another plan.

"I don't like noise either, Mr. Hayes."

"The grinding sound, like rusted old gears in my head." He shifted in the seat, a sign of his growing agitation. Still, he went on speaking, his tone pleasantly conversational despite the gasoline fumes. It was as if he was on the porch talking with guests, the shy smile playing over his mouth as he glanced at her across the back of the seat.

"During the summer there had been several attacks on women, and Miss Palmer didn't want to come with me to my room. Eventually I persuaded the young lady to go with me to get away from those terrible sounds. We were in my room for a while, but then she refused to consider a trip to the dunes. I left her sleeping contentedly, and I went off to set the fires."

"You set the fires."

"Yes. With all the commotion surrounding the spreading flames, those who saw me carrying Miss Palmer—she had fainted I told the one or two who asked—believed I was a hero, taking her to safety.

I lost her purse. I heard it had been found. It's amazing, isn't it?"

Mr. Hayes opened his bloody mouth in a silent laugh.

Eden asked about the cabin fire at the lodge.

"I heard shots, and I went to investigate. Your aunt was visible through the window. Even from a distance I concluded there was nothing I could do for her." He chuckled. "I've had experience with dying and death, you see.

"The shooter had left by the time I arrived. I never saw who it was. In any case, I'd been thinking about incinerating the place for several years, and I took advantage of the opportunity presented. I couldn't stand it for another summer, the appalling noise when Cap was transporting his filthy drugs. And entertaining women."

"You told me earlier tonight you hadn't planned on ever returning to the lodge. Why bother with the fire?"

"At the time I burned the cabin, I had to take action in order to have any peace upon my then-planned return next year."

The freshening wind through the palms made a stiff rattling like little bones. Gasoline fumes hung in the air. The cooling engine made pinging sounds.

"Let's visit Lily and Jess's graves," Eden said. She spoke in a gentle tone as if Mr. Hayes was a close friend she was inviting to accompany her to her relatives' burial plots.

"Through no fault of my own I had to leave Jess behind because Johnny was coming back. By the time I returned, she had been carried off somewhere." Mr. Hayes said this defensively, as though he was being severely criticized for failure to complete a job. He paused. "But I did bury Miss Palmer."

"Where?"

"Miss Palmer is nearby, where I watched all of you, except for her, of course, at your parties years ago. Her grave is on the north side. It is deep down, covered with shrubs and vines and trees, quite lovely for a resting place but making it a challenge for me to get in there.

"She was a tiny thing, though, like your little friend Raynell, and I was able to carry her in making a few trips. I was strong once. And appealing.

"The problem was they did not want to be with me."

He bowed his head. "Sometimes I feel a terrible cold. An emptiness."

"I think I understand, Mr. Hayes. I have felt it in my own life. The coldness you speak of. The emptiness. It is fear. It comes over me when I am afraid of always being alone."

He wiped his eyes with a handkerchief and glanced at her across the seat back. His eyes were like sockets in a skull.

"Take my hand, Mr. Hayes, and we will visit Miss Palmer."

He gazed through the windshield, considering. "You want to trick me into untying you. Then you will run. You will abandon me."

"You will need to trust me." As she spoke, she finished loosening the rope from her wrists.

"Since you showed an interest in me and my work, I will oblige. To begin, we shall make a fire. It is possible to have a fire even when conditions are wet."

Mr. Hayes shoved the driver's door open and stepped from the car, his back to her. The Chevy was without working interior lights. With her hands freed, she was able to remove the belt from around her neck, undetected.

She waited, unmoving in the shadows as he wrestled with the rear door on the driver's side. When it failed to open, he strode to the other side. There he paused to look out at the sea.

Eden hurled her full weight against the rear door he had moments before struggled with. At the same time she pushed down on its handle. The door made a sharp sound like ice cracking.

"Bitch," he yelled. In a fury he wrenched open the rear door and crawled in, his fists ready to batter her. He had forgotten his butcher knife on the front seat. Eden was ready for him. She raked the belt buckle across his eyes, drawing blood. He screamed with pain.

His face a mask of blood and raw flesh, he lunged at her as she threw her body against the door one last time.

Eden sprawled to the ground, then scrambled to her feet. Bobby Hayes crouched on the backseat with his head bowed, moaning. She withdrew the Golden Cove Hotel matchbook from a pocket of her dress, tore out and lit one match and used it to light all that remained, quickly dropping the burning matchbook into the car. She ran into the wilderness.

She did not look back. The thunder of the surf drew her through the dunes wilderness to the shore. Palmetto boughs with razor-sharp leaves sliced her flesh. Her feet ached from stepping on woody branches and shells.

Suddenly the night with its stars and its deep spaces between the stars looked down on Eden. And there was the sea rolling toward her as though coming to take her home.

She plunged into the water and swam through the heavy surf, pulling air into her lungs and diving under huge swells. In a lull between sets of waves, she raised one arm, bringing it forward, down, and back, then the other arm, moving away from the pier and the shore. She swam in the direction of Red Parker's Reef.

When exhaustion overcame her and she could not go any farther, she stopped and waited to draw her last breath and sink beneath the waves. She looked toward the dunes wilderness one last time. From the clearing, flames rose into the night sky.

Inside the flames, she saw the hulk of the Chevy. Figures moved around it, their movements unhurried as they doused the blaze. Beyond the burning car she glimpsed the flashing lights of an ambulance slowly moving to the main road. Its siren was silent. There was no need to rush to the hospital with its gruesome cargo.

Gasoline and fire were so familiar to Mr. Hayes he had thought nothing of it when the container of flammable liquid overturned, soaking the car. He had thought the gasoline was his friend. The fire would destroy Eden's butchered corpse but would not touch him.

He had been wrong.

She rode a wave to the shore and crawled from the sea onto the wet sand. Something was moving at the base of the dunes. Its bones and blood, its fur, these carried the scent of the wind and the sea, of darkness and moonlight, rain and the heat of the sun. In the west, the moon slipped behind the clouds and the fox slipped away into the wilderness.

Chapter Forty

Birds sailed overhead. The boat rocked gently on slow rolling swells. From her backpack Eden removed a container and set it beside her. She unfastened a silver chain from around her neck and held it in the palm of her hand. She spoke out loud: "Jess, this necklace is from your daughter, Raynell, and from me. Raynell will come here to the reef one day, after she has learned from her daddy about you being her mama and CJ her granddaddy. Cyril will tell Raynell about you, Jess, and about CJ before she is old enough to come here to dive the reef. By then, she'll have learned this is a sacred place because you and CJ are buried here, like both of you would have wanted."

Several days earlier, a team of divers had found human bones at Red Parker's near the Corsair. The remains had not yet been identified, but Eden knew Jess's spirit was here. She was going to make sure CJ would join her. Lily would too, when they found her.

Eden held the canister over the edge of the boat, releasing CJ's ashes into the water. Then she released the chain and its heart-shaped pendant. It sank through the pale light. A school of dolphins broke through the waves. A flight of pelicans flew overhead. She pulled up anchor and headed into shore.

By early afternoon she was surfing beyond the pier at the fox dunes. She wanted to enjoy the moment, say farewell to the past, and think about the future. Scooter's body had been found in the new pickup abandoned across from the lodge during the storm. Johnny was wanted for the murder. Eden wondered if she'd ever see Johnny again.

For one thing, Scooter's boat was gone. She thought it likely Johnny's life at sea would involve a search for a place of rest and peace. She hoped he would find it one day. Eden closed her eyes, and Johnny walked toward her along a mountain pass. Snow was falling.

A wave lifted the board beneath her. Jess's voice came to her in the wind from over the dunes. She heard Luke's voice in the roll of the waves. Hearing her sister and brother urging her on, Eden stood tall on her board, moving forward with the wave toward the beach.

She reached the shallows where she jumped off and hauled the board out of the water, then dropped onto the wet sand. Her body was achingly tired. Her skin burned with the sun and intense heat of the day.

Someone was coming toward her from up the beach.

"You rode a wave all the way."

"You sound surprised." Eden gazed into the pitted face with its scar across the forehead.

He set his board beside hers. "Not at all. I knew you would do it. All you needed was a few lessons from a superior teacher. And practice. Practice makes perfect, Eden. I think you have learned this valuable lesson."

Eden gave him a sharp glance in time to see the corners of his mouth move. He was not used to smiling, and it vanished as quickly as it had appeared. It was enough, though, for her to sense in his smile something adventurous.

They climbed on their boards and headed out. It was one of those times where she didn't think it possible, but she found the reserves of energy she needed after all. Even if they paddled clear to the shipping lane, she would be able to get there and back.

And there was something else she could handle.

"Are you married, McCabe?"

"Was. She left us. I have custody of my daughter, Emma."

"The child in the photo?"

"Yes. She was with her aunt, my sister Helen. She lives with her."

He must have sensed it would take more evidence to convince Eden. "You are going to meet her. You'll stay with them, of course." Same old McCabe. Eden sighed.

When the wave came hurtling toward them, Eden and McCabe were ready for it. They rode it all the way in side by side.

They walked to the clearing and the battered Silverado parked there waiting for them.

***

Eden was thinking McCabe would step past the bus terminal door onto the platform at any second with the bottled water she had sent him for. To one side of the door, a Navy recruitment poster showed a young woman about Eden's age in uniform. A series of smaller pictures, displaying career opportunities, surrounded the young woman. Eden found herself drawn to the one showing a woman at the controls of a helicopter landing on a ship.

McCabe came through the door with the cold bottled water for Eden and Raynell. The liquid felt good sliding down her throat.

"Eden, I wish you'd let me take you and Raynell in the Cessna. In fact, you could fly us. You'll be there in no time."

"Try telling Raynell. She's excited about the trip. Something about wanting to get pictures of semitrailer trucks."

McCabe set his hands on his hips and looked at Raynell with a puzzled expression. "Big rigs?"

Raynell gave him a vigorous nod. She said, "I'm particularly interested in photographing motion at this point in my career."

McCabe said, "I never gave them much thought, but since you've brought them to my attention, I'd like to see some of the pictures you're going to take of eighteen-wheelers on the move."

Raynell said, "Eden likes them, too."

McCabe, with an eye on Eden, pulled from his pocket a wad of cash and counted out ten hundred-dollar bills. First it had been Scooter. Then McCabe. Men were offering her money these days. Which was a good thing. Eventually she wouldn't need to worry, and neither would Ruth or Raynell. But at present, the money flow hadn't straightened itself out.

There were bank accounts they had inherited along with the Fox Dunes Lodge and its land at Magnolia Beach, as well as property in Miami, Orlando, and Jacksonville. All of it had been properly documented and witnessed in the Florida land trust CJ had set up to avoid making his holdings public in the courts.

Eden thought about how close she'd come to overlooking the notebooks Jess had hidden in her closet. She thought about the time she'd spent trying to understand the papers she'd found at CJ's. Based on their tattered condition, she believed CJ at one time probably intended to throw them out but never got around to it.

Ruth would make the lodge her home for as long as she wanted. It was Eden's home, too. But how much time she would spend there was hard to say. There was restlessness in her.

She knew one day the land would be home to plants and animals, the wind, sun and moon, the stars. The other land willed to them would also be conserved.

"It's a loan," McCabe said when Eden didn't take the cash he held out to her. But with a glance at Raynell, she reconsidered the offer.

"Thanks, McCabe." She took the bills and slipped them in her pocket.

He was studying the people flowing around them. Eden wondered what his trained eye was looking for or what he saw, but she suspected he'd give his life for her and Raynell. This is what they did in the military. He had taken her and Raynell for a tour of the base where he was on temporary duty, to the north of the lodge.

Raynell glanced from McCabe to Eden. She pulled a book from her backpack, walked a few feet from where they were standing, set the backpack down, and settled comfortably on top of it. The child opened the book and flipped to its first page.

"Well, so long, and thanks for everything," Eden said. He had spoken of having her meet his sister, but he'd also volunteered for another tour of duty in the Middle East and could be called to go at any time. Too many good men had never returned.

"The surfing lessons were helpful," she said.

"You taught yourself. I hope I don't need to remind you to keep at it, Eden. And you can't use being in Illinois as an excuse. I heard there's surfing on Lake Michigan even in winter. I'll be in Chicago for training in a couple of weeks. If the surf's up, want to go?"

Eden told him yes.

Before she knew what was happening, Eden and McCabe had stepped into each other's arms. Her cheek pressed his, and she breathed in his scent of faraway places.

Their lips met as she felt a tug at her sleeve.

"The bus is leaving," Raynell said. They managed to get the last seats available together, and they settled in. Raynell sat next to the window.

The bus rocked as it moved out of the depot and turned one corner, then another. The streets steamed from a recent rain. Ragged palms swayed in the wind and slanting light. The bus rolled onto the highway and gained speed.

Raynell took pictures of the tractor-trailers sliding by. Later, after Raynell had fallen asleep, Eden pulled a sweater from her backpack and set it around the child's fragile shoulders. Eden closed her eyes. And before long she saw a girl with a fox at her side running toward the waves and the sun rising above Red Parker's Reef.

The End